She paused to ac room Nick's interior designer sister, created. Thank goodness she'd chosen to stow most of her belongings in storage.

Even without her furniture, she'd crammed the moving truck with her favorite paintings and pictures, too many boxes of books to count—as luck would have it, Christian had the brawn to lug them all in—and all her clothes. And shoes.

"Where do you want the boxes of bricks?" His raspy voice sounded from behind her.

She turned, and he was framed in the doorway, his defined biceps bulging with two hefty book cartons stacked under his chin. He quirked a dark brow. He'd pushed the sunglasses back onto his thick deep brown hair, and his eyes glowed a sparkling mossy green. A different color from the last time she saw them. Her lips parted, and her mind blanked.

"Anytime. They only weigh about fifty pounds." Not a hint of a smile.

"Sorry, sorry. How about against the far wall in the living room, under the window? Actually, all the book boxes can go there. Wardrobe boxes in the bedroom. Obviously." Her cheeks heated when she said bedroom. Geez, what was wrong with her? He was just really, really hot.

He crossed the polished hardwood floor, set the boxes down under the enormous picture window, and headed back to the truck without a word.

Praise for Claire Marti

"Sweet, sexy, lush, and lovely, this series is a new force in the genre you won't be able to put down until the ultimately satisfying end..."

~ Kerrigan Byrne, Bestselling author
of the Victorian Rebels series

"Readers are intrigued right from the very start of At Last in Laguna...Powerful characters and an unusual conundrum plus plenty of hot action make this a top choice read for any romance fan."

~ Long and Short Reviews.

Sunset in Laguna

by

Claire Marti

Finding Forever in Laguna

Sunset in Laguna

Cover Art by *RJ Morris*

The Wild Rose Press, Inc.
PO Box 708
Adams Basin, NY 14410-0708
Visit us at www.thewildrosepress.com

Publishing History
First Champagne Rose Edition, 2018
Print ISBN 978-1-5092-2092-2
Digital ISBN 978-1-5092-2093-9

Finding Forever in Laguna
Published in the United States of America

Dedication

To my one and only love.

Acknowledgements

Several people helped me to create well-researched characters and bring Christian and Kelly's story to life. In order to make Kelly's role as a lawyer seeking justice against a corrupt client as realistic as possible, I was lucky enough to consult with attorney-extraordinaire Jaime Moss, who provided me with keen insight and helpful advice. I want to thank Retired U.S. Army Special Forces Lieutenant Colonel Mitch Utterback for sharing his expertise about all things military. Christian Wolfe's authenticity stems from your vast and varied experiences.

I want to thank my wonderful beta readers and critique partners. Kay Bennett, Lacy Pope, Joanna Kelly, Leslie Hachtel, April Fink, and Kerrigan Byrne—you each help me more than you could imagine. I appreciate your time and opinions.

Thank you to everyone at The Wild Rose Press for believing in me as an author and launching my career with my Finding Forever in Laguna series. To my wonderful editor, Roseann Armstrong, thanks for helping me become a better writer.

Last but not least, to Todd for being the best husband in the world. I love you. And finally, to my furry kids: Josie, Lola, and Beau. Thanks for providing me unconditional love.

Chapter 1

Christian Wolfe squeezed his eyes shut, willing the sharp pain piercing his temples to dissipate. A nasty force tightened the screws of the vise around his skull, and he marveled his eyes didn't pop out of his head. He sucked in a few deep breaths to steady himself. Would these headaches ever stop kicking his ass?

Cracking open one eye, he closed the accounting file with a decisive click. Business was excellent at Vines, the wine bar he owned. Despite having a bookkeeper, he couldn't help double-checking the numbers.

Once a control freak, always a control freak.

He surged to his feet and gripped the edge of his sturdy mahogany desk. Fresh air. Outdoors. Even though sunlight could exacerbate the pain, his trusty mirrored aviator sunglasses helped. Where were they? Why the hell weren't they in their usual spot in the tray on the top left corner of his desk?

Amber, his exceedingly competent bar manager, entered his office. "Christian, can you—"

"Not now. Sorry." He held up one hand once he spotted the glasses on the top right corner of the desk.

She stepped aside, silent, and he skirted around her to exit the building pronto. She'd seen him bolt out of the restaurant a few times and was always discreet. Probably why he liked her so much.

He stalked toward the beach in the center of town.

Each inhalation of the salty ocean air softened the iron tendrils clutching his skull. Damn it, something needed to change. He couldn't keep running out of the wine bar every time his head hurt—and it hurt like hell—or when panic bubbled to the surface. Vines would go out of business, and he wasn't prepared to surrender his new civilian life.

Many of his army buddies were surprised when he'd decided to open a wine bar instead of pushing paper for the government. But he'd had enough of war and bureaucracy. Besides, he had a soft spot for his grandmother, who'd come over from Italy when she'd been a young girl. Sharing delicious food and fine wine was a nod to his heritage. And running a successful business gratified him. Taking charge, organizing, and pouring wine weren't exactly saving the world, but too bad.

He arrived at the small beach, stopped on the promenade, and stared out at the white-capped waves of the Pacific. Although he wasn't as avid a surfer as his buddies Nick and Brandt, he enjoyed the adrenaline rush from riding waves. Mostly, he loved how the salt air acted like a balm, soothing his pounding head. Especially when he felt amped and anxious, like now.

Something needed to change. Support groups and doctors didn't help. No more discussing the horrors of losing some of his men and watching others lose limbs or worse. No more talking about the failed rogue mission on his first tour. Definitely no reviving the crushing losses suffered by his Iraqi counterparts on the subsequent three trips back to the Middle East.

When he resigned his commission, the doctors proclaimed his headaches and nightmares were symptoms of posttraumatic stress. Screw that. He squeezed his eyes shut, blocking out Laguna Beach's postcard view, and willed his shoulders to relax.

About six months ago, Amber had left a pamphlet for Peaceful Warrior, a local veterans' organization, by his computer. He'd skimmed it. Pondered the various offerings. None appealed except for the meditation classes.

Although he knew where the center was, he'd avoided checking it out. Yet the meditation group intrigued him. Could it really help him quell the panic attacks? Someone had described meditation as learning to control your mind or direct your thoughts to where you want them to go. Running from the nightmares and stress obviously wasn't working for him.

He kept his eyes shut, savoring the warmth of the sun on his skin, and continued to drink in the crisp ocean air—this was as close to meditating as he'd ever achieved. Hell, he'd check out the schedule now. Nobody needed to know. But he'd be damned if he'd wear flowy white pants, sniff incense, or hold those fancy beads that resembled a rosary from his Catholic-elementary-school days.

He spun away from the comfort of the azure waves and walked the few blocks to Peaceful Warrior. The tree-lined street was quiet. The pedestrians and tourists tended to flock to the main drag. Nonetheless, he glanced over his right shoulder, then flicked his gaze to the left. Double-checked the right side again. Nobody around. He wasn't paranoid. Just cautious.

He approached the older brick building and hesitated a few paces in front of the entrance. Took a step back and considered the unimposing two-story facade. He stood taller, assuming his military posture.

Maybe he just needed a punishing session with the punching bag or a few fingers of Jameson whiskey. *Stop being such a damn wuss.* Workouts and alcohol weren't driving the demons away. He stepped forward. Something needed to change.

"Christian?" A husky voice lilted his name.

His head whipped to the right. A beautiful woman dressed in a conservative dark suit and tortoiseshell glasses stared at him. Somewhere in his brain he registered dangerously toned legs encased in red skyscraper-high stilettos.

Sweat popped onto his brow, and he swallowed, his throat suddenly parched. Recognition flooded his system when he dragged his gaze up from those spiked heels. Her tawny cat eyes captured his—Kelly Prescott. Didn't she live in San Diego?

"Um, hey, Kelly." What the hell was she doing at Peaceful Warrior?

"What are you—?"

"Why are you—?"

"Ladies first." Distract. Deflect. Damn it to hell.

"Well, it's kind of a secret at the moment, but I'm about to interview for the general counsel position here." The corners of her rosy lips curved up.

"General counsel?" For some reason he couldn't seem to utter more than two words at a time.

"Yes. They've needed one for a long time and recently got a grant to fund it. So here I am." She walked toward him. Hints of cinnamon and some exotic scent assaulted his nostrils.

He drew in his abs and expanded his chest. Kind of like a rooster. He grunted. "You're going to commute?"

"No, if I get the job, I'm actually moving up here." She shrugged and flashed perfect white teeth, oblivious of his discomfort.

"Huh." Over a year ago, her golden beauty had caught his attention when she'd accompanied his buddy Nick and Sophie to Vines. He'd been single at the time—hell, he was always single—and asked Nick about her. She was Sophie's best friend. His attraction cooled when he'd learned she was a wealthy corporate attorney working for her daddy's firm and dating another lawyer. Too complicated.

"So what are you doing here?" She tilted her head up, still about a foot shorter than he was, even with those damn shoes that would be forever burned into his brain.

"Oh, just taking a break from work, getting some fresh air." He gestured with palms sweatier than they'd ever been in the searing heat of the Middle East.

"Funny, I thought you were going inside too." She raised perfectly groomed eyebrows. "Wish me luck?"

"Good luck." Apparently, he'd never speak in full sentences again. His brain waves sputtered and sparked, nothing igniting except for a curl of lust in his gut.

"Thanks. Are you sure you don't want to go in?" Her eyes were the color of burnt caramel—stunning.

"No." Had he yelled? "No, thanks. I'll just finish my walk."

A good soldier knew when to retreat. He pivoted abruptly and strode in the opposite direction of his wine bar. He expelled a deep breath and wiped his damp hands on his jeans.

Although he'd managed to avoid discussing why he was lurking outside of Peaceful Warrior, he couldn't remember a word he'd said. Damn it, she'd totally thrown him off guard. Images of sliding those glasses off her pert little nose and wrapping his hands in her long sun-streaked hair assaulted him.

He prayed the walk would cool him off. If not, he'd need to dive into the frigid Pacific Ocean.

Chapter 2

Kelly closed the door behind her and sagged back against it, fanning her face with one hand. Her cheeks were burning from what could only be described as a strange encounter with the tall, dark, and smoldering Christian Wolfe. Up close, he was quite the specimen. Pure animal attraction—it was the only logical answer. Lord knows his conversational skills left something to be desired.

What had he been doing in front of Peaceful Warrior? She shook her head. Not her problem. She had enough of her own at the moment, thank you very much. She entered the office doorway into a cramped, deserted reception area and double-checked her watch. The brief conversation had only cost her three minutes. She was still early.

She tapped the toe of her scarlet patent-leather stiletto on the linoleum floor and checked her watch for the hundredth time. Her appointment was at one thirty, and it was already two fifteen. At least her overheated skin had cooled.

She glowered at the Executive Director nameplate on the battered office door, willing the occupant to open it and meet with her already. Damn it, she'd played hooky from the office, and the last thing she needed was her father lecturing her on the importance of billable hours. This interview symbolized more than a new job. It represented a complete life reset.

Without warning, the executive director's door flew open. Kelly straightened her spine and smoothed back an errant strand of hair determined to escape her low chignon.

"Ms. Prescott?" A stocky red-faced man with steel-wool hair barked at her, pinning her with dark raisin eyes. His short-sleeved olive-green golf shirt and khaki slacks didn't exactly shout "executive."

Accustomed to snarling bosses, she nodded and rose from the hard plastic chair. She strode toward him and shook his hand. "Kelly Prescott and you must be Mr. Williams."

"Come on in, come on in." He turned, and she followed him into a musty shoebox of an office. Banker cartons lined the walls from the dingy beige carpet to the low popcorn ceiling. A small window could have offered some natural light and fresh air, but battered vinyl blinds prevented relief for the oppressive room. The warm air was as still as a tomb. If this were the executive director's office, would she be assigned a closet?

He gestured to an old-fashion armless office chair in the midst of the chaos. She sat, carefully placed her red leather briefcase on the floor, folded her hands in her lap, and struggled to regulate her pounding heart. The nerves were solely based on the stakes of the interview and had nothing to do with Christian Wolfe. Nothing at all.

He leaned against the edge of an enormous weathered-oak desk and crossed hefty arms across a barrel-like chest. Was that a Rolodex on his desk? It couldn't be, could it? Did he have a typewriter too? *Pay attention, girl.*

"So tell me why I should hire you." His face was impassive.

"Well, I'm confident I'm the best fit for the general counsel position. I've got a history of excelling at whatever I do, starting with graduating summa cum—"

"I've read your resume. I know you're smart. You work for the Prescott Law Firm. Your dad's got a reputation, so I figure you're tough. Tell me what I don't know." He shook his head.

She paused and pushed her glasses back up onto the bridge of her nose. So he didn't want to hear about the high-profile cases she'd won. Already this was a complete one-eighty from her comfort zone in the big bad world of corporate litigation. Thank goodness. Time to shift gears. She squared her shoulders.

"You're correct. I'm smart. I'm tough. I'm not afraid of hard work. What my resume doesn't show is that I care. I want to work somewhere I'll make a difference. Where I can actually help people instead of making huge corporations more money." Where justice and compassion are valued, not irrelevant.

"Okay, that explains nonprofit. Why work with veterans? Why Peaceful Warrior?" His neutral tone revealed nothing.

"Because I care about the people who've served our country. They should be treated as heroes and given the chance to start over. New careers. New lives." She inhaled deeply, warming to the topic. "I've researched your foundation, and I love what you do. It's important. It's vital. We need more organizations dedicated to providing assistance to these displaced soldiers—"

"This is more of a jack-of-all-trades than a

traditional attorney role. It's tough. The money sucks. It's not about billable hours. It takes a personal connection." He raised a bushy brow. "What's yours?"

"My roommate in college was ROTC and served in Iraq after graduation. She died, and her family was devastated. I ended up reading more about all the problems with the people who actually do return home and can't seem to reintegrate." She leaned forward, her hands gripping her thighs, her gaze intent upon his. She wouldn't allow him to throw her off with constant interruptions—she was used to them.

"I'm also experienced with trying to help someone I care about beat addiction. I know how much support troubled people need." Her stomach clenched, and she blinked to keep her eyes from filling.

He frowned and shook his head. "This isn't a group of addicts, Ms. Prescott. Far from it. Sure, some of the soldiers are struggling with booze and drugs, but it's just one small segment of what we do."

"Of course, I know the focus is on helping vets and their families with a variety of issues from legal to medical to finding housing or a job and providing complimentary programs like meditation." Crap, had she screwed this up already? Her belly certainly wouldn't unwind.

"So the big question is can you handle it without becoming too emotionally entangled?" Doubt crept into his baritone voice.

"Are you too emotionally entangled, sir?" Frost cut through her tone, and she pressed her lips together. If one more person implied being a woman would impact her professionalism, she would scream.

"Touché. I'm not trying to be a hard-ass. Well,

twenty-five years in the Marines will do that to you. This is another world compared to big corporate law." He paused and shrugged. "You'll be handling a lot of the business stuff, but we're small. A lot of this is personal. You'll meet people with stories that would rip apart even the hardest of hearts. And you need to project calm for them no matter what. They can't doubt your capability."

She nodded. "I get it. Look, I've got a great poker face. I was assigned the more challenging clients because of my ability to stay calm." On the surface anyway. If anybody could read her mind or hear her galloping heart...

He scrunched his brows together, unconvinced. "Well, I'm—"

"Mr. Williams, I am the perfect person for this job. Do you have any other objections to bringing me on?" She leaned forward, injecting strength and confidence into her tone, her lawyer voice.

"Did you look at the salary? We received a grant to cover it, which is why we've actually got this new position. Your office would be so small it makes mine look like the Taj Mahal, a lot of the work isn't attorney work, and if you think you billed a lot of hours before, you'll do more here without a whiff of a year-end bonus."

"Yes, I did." She nodded and struggled to breathe evenly. "The salary is...um...low. I'm not afraid of long hours. I've planned an appropriate budget." She'd squirreled away most of her generous salary to escape a life she hadn't chosen.

Enough was enough. For the last six months, she'd cried every morning in the shower, dreading going to work in her overbearing father's stuffy, possibly corrupt, law firm. Time to create her life on her own terms.

"Don't you live in San Diego? You're willing to move?" He crossed his arms over his chest again.

"For now. I've got a lead on a place here." Her belly leapt in anticipation. Sophie would rent her the cottage, wouldn't she?

"When could you start?"

"Are you offering me the job?" She gripped the edges of the chair to stop herself before she bounced in her seat like a little kid.

"Ms. Prescott, would you be interested in becoming the general counsel for Peaceful Warrior?" Finally, he smiled.

"Absolutely." She returned his smile, stood, and resisted the urge to hug him. "Absolutely."

He stepped forward and grasped her hand, a stronger, warmer handshake than before. Had her entire life just changed in the course of a quarter hour?

"When can you start? As you can see, we're a little backed up around here." He gestured to the mountains of documents stuffed into the room.

"Can you give me a few weeks? I need to resign and move. And I could commute at first because I'm in Solana Beach in North County San Diego, and it isn't far."

"Of course. What's a few more weeks? We'll get all the paperwork handled, and I'll have Susan clear out your office and get it set up."

"Susan?" Was she the one who manned the lobby desk buried in messy piles of loose paper, manila folders, and an antiquated desktop computer covered in pink and yellow sticky notes?

"She's my, well now, our assistant. She's probably back. She's a tough old bird, but I'm sure you'll be able to charm her." He moved behind his desk and dropped his bulk into his chair.

"*Old bird*?" Seriously?

"Ha, ha. Susan is my wife, and it's a pet name. I'm the old goat. Look, we aren't formal here. If you're going to be upset anytime something isn't politically correct, you should really think about your decision." He drummed his fingers on the desk.

"No, no, I'm fine. Just not used to it, that's all." She swallowed a laugh. If her father had ever referred to her mother as an old bird, well…

"Great. Let's have a start date of two weeks from Monday, okay? I'll have her email you over all the employment paperwork." His attention shifted to the chaos on his desk.

"Yes, please. Thank you so much. I'm thrilled to be coming on board." Her heart started racing again. She picked up her briefcase and navigated through the tunnel of boxes to the lobby.

The reception area remained empty. She paused and scanned the shabby room that would be her new home away from home. Vital energy surged through her veins. She'd succeeded in the first stage of her plan. She'd worry about resigning and facing her father's wrath later.

Time to call Sophie and share the news. Her best friend didn't know she was in town but would be thrilled for her. After all, Sophie had found a second chance in Laguna, so why couldn't she?

Chapter 3

Kelly parked in front of Vines, unable to wipe off the grin plastered across her face. It was time to celebrate the biggest transition of her life. Luckily, Sophie's author schedule was flexible. They'd toast with one flute of bubbly before she returned to the drama in San Diego. Why not?

She flicked off the engine of her sensible sedan and checked her reflection in the mirror. Her cheeks were still flushed. Certainly, it was due to all the excitement about her new career. Absolutely nothing to do with the run-in with Christian. Nothing at all.

She opened the car door and waved at Sophie, who strode across the pedestrian crosswalk toward her. Her friend looked as cute as ever, with her dark hair flowing over her shoulders and the glow of happiness shining from her flawless features.

"Perfect timing. It's so good to see you." Sophie wrapped her slender arms around her and squeezed.

"You too. Thanks so much for coming out in the middle of the day. I appreciate it." She reveled in the warmth emanating from her best friend, the person she trusted most in the world, her true sister.

"One of the perks of being my own boss. I'm thrilled to see you and curious why you're here in the middle of the day in a fancy dark suit. Spill it."

"Let's sit down first, and I'll fill you in." She

grabbed Sophie's hand, and they entered the wine bar together.

Although it wasn't happy hour yet, several tables were occupied and a handful of people lounged on the leather barstools. The ocean breeze flowed in through the wide stainless-steel garage-style windows, and the high wood-beamed ceiling imparted 'a sense of openness.

"Bar or table?" Sophie asked as they crossed the room toward the long polished mahogany bar framed by an exposed brick wall.

"Table, please. I've got some things to discuss, and I want to keep it private." Her belly jumped with nerves. Come to think of it, the butterflies had ratcheted up after her encounter with the sexy Christian Wolfe.

"Are you okay? Is it Robert?" Sophie halted midstride.

"No, no. Definitely not Robert. You know we've been broken up for months. This is serious." For some reason it didn't seem weird to dismiss two years with Robert as not serious. Oh well.

They chose a table near the enormous windows and hung their purses on the small brass hooks under the gleaming wood tabletop. A statuesque redhead approached them with menus and a wide grin.

"Hey, Sophie, taking a break from all the writing?" The woman's tone was friendly.

"Exactly, Amy." Sophie laughed. "This is my friend Kelly, and we'd love some champagne."

"Nice to meet you, Kelly. Did you ladies want a bottle of the Cristal?"

"Nice to meet you too." Kelly shook her head and returned the smile. "I'm driving back to San Diego, so just a glass."

Sophie focused her gaze on Kelly. "Okay, what are we celebrating? What are you doing here?"

"I'll give you three guesses." Suddenly relaxed, she propped her chin in her hand and held up three fingers.

"You're running away to Africa to study lions? Traveling to Ireland to open a pub? Auditioning for the ballet?" Sophie's big sapphire-blue eyes were wide, her tongue firmly planted in her cheek.

"Oh yes, because I'm so graceful, definitely the ballet." She paused. "Okay, guessing won't work with your overly imaginative writer's brain. I just accepted a job at Peaceful Warrior as general counsel. I'm quitting the firm and moving up here. Well, moving up here if you'll rent me the cottage?" The words tumbled out in a whoosh. Nothing like throwing it all out on the table.

"What? What?" Sophie jumped out of her chair and grabbed Kelly's hands, pulling her up too. They jumped up and down and hugged again. "But how? What? What's with the secretiveness? Who are you, and what did you do with my must-have-a-plan best friend?" Sophie shifted back and peered at her.

"Okay, okay. Let's sit down, and I'll fill you in. You know I'm not creative like you. I'm anal. Logical. Like to have all my ducks in a row before I make a move." *Because I've never really made a move.*

"You mean like getting a new job in a new field in a new city without telling a soul? Moving? No, not impulsive at all," Sophie joked.

"Yes, I'm done. Done, done, done. I'll explain more later, but the most recent case I've been working on was the straw that broke this camel's back. I just can't do it anymore." She thumped her hand on the table. She could not and would not do it anymore.

"I'm excited for you. You've felt like an imposter in your role there since you started. Pulling the trigger is the right thing to do. And, of course, you can rent the cottage. I'll even give you a special price." Sophie waggled her eyebrows.

They paused for a moment when Amy returned with the flutes of sparkling liquid and a dish of delicious Marcona almonds.

"Perfect. Thank you." She picked up her glass and clinked her best friend's. She sipped the cool crisp liquid and closed her eyes in pleasure as it slid down her throat. "So your following your dreams helped me admit to myself I was living a lie... No more double life. I want to help people with my law degree, not destroy them, damn it."

"So why Peaceful Warrior?" Sophie nodded and gestured with her glass for her to continue.

"Don't laugh, but I made a vision board. Well, more of a color-coded spreadsheet, but still. I'm looking for the intersection of my personal preferences and my professional skills. Connecting the dots."

"Rational and smart. Just like you." Sophie's eyes sparkled. She held up her hand. "Toast, then more."

They clinked glasses and took another sip.

"General counsel for a nonprofit is a perfect fit. Standing up for those who truly need help. No more billable hours. More contractual work, less litigation." A smile spread across her face. She wasn't talking about it anymore. She was doing it.

"A place where you can fix things. Fix people. Help." Sophie nodded and nibbled an almond.

"Exactly. I'm not afraid of long hours, but I need to

be able to look myself in the mirror in the morning and be okay. I haven't felt that way in a long time." Since she'd been sworn in to the California Bar and worked for her father?

"I know. And I know the situation with Robert doesn't help. Having to see him at work every day and know he's a simpering little weasel sucking up to your dad can't be easy." Sophie frowned.

"Pfffft." She waved her hand. "He's the least of my concerns." Weasel was right.

"Good. He never deserved you." Sophie frowned. "I love that you'll be able to use all the empathy you've wasted on your family and your job. With your wicked legal skills, you'll change the world."

Yes, she damn well would change the world. Too bad she wasn't staying in town overnight because another glass of champagne definitely appealed. She clinked her rapidly emptying glass with Sophie's.

"Have you planned what to say to your dad?"

"Umm...no." Her stomach dropped. "I'm dreading it. I'm going to try to keep it businesslike—just a straightforward I'm resigning. I've accepted this new job and deal with it. What can he do?"

What couldn't Alistair Prescott III do? A ruthless adversary, a skilled businessman, an unemotional father, he did whatever he wanted. In order to survive her childhood and professional life, she'd built up armor. But she'd never tested it by truly crossing him. Who knew how he would react at what he'd view as a betrayal?

"Well, your dad is...tough." Sophie ran her tongue over her teeth. "Do you want me to come down for moral support? I'm happy to."

"You're too sweet. No, I need to handle this myself. How bad can it be?" She shuddered. Who was she kidding? His bite was as bad as his bark.

"Oh, there's Christian." Sophie popped up out of her chair again and waved him over.

Kelly whipped her head up, and his tiger eyes snared her gaze as he approached their table. Awareness prickled along her spine, and her belly tightened in a very different way than a few minutes ago. He looked like Heathcliff sauntering into the twenty-first century. Hot.

"Sophie, good to see you." He hugged her best friend, his bronzed muscular arms flexing.

"You too. You remember my best friend, Kelly. You guys were in the wedding party together." Sophie smiled at them, unaware of Kelly's sudden discomfort.

"Hey." His cool gaze flicked toward her for a split second before he shifted it back to Sophie. "I've got work to do. Champagne's on me, ladies." He turned and strode toward the office behind the bar.

"What's his deal?" Kelly couldn't suppress the note of annoyance in her voice. Come to think of it, he'd barely spoken to her at Nick and Sophie's wedding either. She hadn't thought much of it at the time because she was contending with Robert's childish behavior.

"Christian? Oh, he's just more comfortable with people he knows well. Don't take it personally." Sophie waved off her question.

"Well, he's kind of rude." Seriously, he'd been friendlier, although monosyllabic, when she'd seen him on the street.

"Don't take it personally." Sophie rubbed her hand.

"Remember the first time you visited after I'd moved and we came here with Nick? You two were making googly eyes at each other from across the room."

"Googly eyes? Please? I may have checked him out—I mean, he's gorgeous and mysterious. And I certainly didn't notice him making eyes at me." Okay, maybe she *was* a teensy bit offended he'd barely glanced at her.

"Well, he most definitely did. He's quiet, but he and Nick are close. Nick says he's a war hero. He was in the Special Forces and did three or four tours in the Middle East."

"Really? I just saw him outside of the Peaceful Warrior office, and he acted strange. Now I really wonder why he was there." Her brain whirred with possibilities. He *had* been planning on going in.

"Outside Peaceful Warrior?" Sophie glanced toward the bar, but Christian had disappeared into his office and closed the door.

"It sure looked like it. He said he'd just been getting some fresh air. Huh?" Her protective instincts jumped to attention.

"You can find out once you move here. Back to your plans." Sophie waved a hand. "I'm so excited we'll be in the same city again. How soon can you move? The cottage is open and furnished, if you don't feel like lugging up your own stuff."

"Well, I agreed to a start date in two weeks. I have to survive the resignation. Then I'm fine with putting most of my furniture in storage. The cottage is adorable, and it'll be a lot easier." The simpler the better.

"Well, if your dad gives you the boot now, you can

come anytime. I'll clean and air it out for you. Also, I can come down and help you pack." Sophie beamed at her.

"Don't you have a deadline for your next book?" She was thrilled at her friend's success. Her debut novel had been a smash, and she'd signed with an agent and had a three-book deal with one of the big New York publishers.

"Yes, but the busier I am, the more I get done. I've been procrastinating a little bit..." Sophie shrugged, and a sheepish expression crossed her face.

"I'll let you know. I should be able to handle it. I'm just nervous. Should I tell my dad tonight or formally at the office tomorrow?" Her belly no longer fluttered over the sexy wine-bar owner. Now it plummeted like an anchor. She grimaced and pressed her hand against the ache.

"Definitely the office. He's less likely to have an epic meltdown at the office." Sophie sounded confident.

Her dad specialized in epic meltdowns at the office. At home. And wherever he liked. She cleared her now-dry throat and contemplated what promised to be an ugly scene. "I've got to get on the road. Thanks so much for meeting me and for all the moral support. I'm doing the right thing, aren't I?" She wouldn't question herself.

"Absolutely. You've got this." Sophie squeezed her hand again.

She hoped her friend was right. They placed the glasses back onto the shiny wood table and left a generous tip for Amy. Before they could head out, the fine hairs on the back of Kelly's neck stood on end. She looked back over her shoulder, and Christian Wolfe stood silhouetted in the doorway behind the bar. She couldn't see his eyes, but the penetrating heat of his gaze seared through her clothes.

Oh, he'd noticed her all right. Satisfaction filled her. But the strong and silent gothic hero could wait.

After another bear hug with Sophie, she hurried to her car. Plenty of time to brood about Mr. Mysterious on the drive back to San Diego. Among a few other choice matters like quitting her job, moving from the only city she'd called home, and confronting her father. Her father didn't handle insubordination from his only child well.

Well, his only living child.

Chapter 4

Kelly woke with a start, bathed in a pool of her own sweat. She'd dreamt the major pharmaceutical company the Prescott Firm represented had kidnapped her, strapped her down, and hooked her to an infusion drip funneling poisonous chemicals into her body. Millions of dollars in profits were at stake, and they'd be damned if one ethical lawyer would get in the way of their moneymaking machine.

Melodramatic?

Actually, not so much. Despite knowing the percentage of cancer diagnoses would be astronomically high, the company had hidden thousands of adverse event reports during the drug's clinical trial phase. They had paid experts to alter clinical data in order to illegally earn FDA drug approval. Despite the known dangers. Despite the certainty it would cause cancer. Maybe the firm's client wouldn't kidnap her, but they'd moved into the realm of fraud, and she had to tell her father.

After the nightmare she'd tossed and turned until she finally forced herself out of her huge nest of a king bed and brewed a punishingly strong pot of coffee and showered. Sipping the steaming drink, she perused the two rows of conservative business suits, organized from light to dark. She selected one of her most conservative suits in dove gray. She always felt a bit invisible in the color, but this morning a cloak of invisibility would be akin to a superpower.

In her cheerful yellow kitchen, she choked down a piece of dry toast. No way could she stomach her usual breakfast of two poached eggs and avocado on whole wheat. She'd eat after seeing her father.

She flew down the 5 Freeway with AC/DC blasting out "Highway to Hell" on the radio and made it to downtown San Diego in nineteen minutes. A personal record. She was a nervous driver and never exceeded the speed limit, but going to the office at six thirty a.m. certainly saved time. Despite the early hour, the security guard was at his post and cleared her entry. Her heels echoed on the dark marble floors of the empty lobby on her way to the bank of elevators. The Prescott firm sprawled over the top four floors of the largest high-rise in San Diego. Of course her father insisted on the most desirable location with sweeping views of the San Diego Harbor, and luxurious offices where no expense had been spared in creating an image of success.

The clientele insisted on it.

The elevator silently shot her to the top floor. She exited and headed toward her soon-to- be-former office. The hallways were empty, and every cubicle deserted. Usually, the secretaries and paralegals arrived anywhere between seven thirty and eight thirty. The attorneys? It all depended on whether they were entertaining clients, going to court, or buried in paperwork.

Bright light blasted through the opening of her slightly ajar office door. Odd. The firm utilized cutting-edge energy-saving lights, and at seven in the morning, they should be on dim.

She pushed the door open and halted in her tracks. "What are you doing in my office?" She struggled to keep her voice calm, although her heart began to hammer.

Robert, her ex-boyfriend and fellow associate attorney, sat at her desk, cozy as you please, with his fingers racing across her computer's keyboard.

"Oh, hey, you're early today. I hope you don't mind, but I couldn't log into my computer and I was just—" He shrugged one shoulder, his expression unruffled, not a strand of his closely cropped light brown hair out of place.

"Oh please. You could use your secretary's computer or one in the library." She strode further into the room and dropped her briefcase down next to her desk.

"It's not a big deal." He leaned back in her chair, as if he had every right to be there.

She circled around the desk. "Why do you have the Hexaun files up? And how did you get my login?" Temper began to lick in her belly.

He swiveled and stood. He was short. When they'd been dating, she'd hated to admit it bothered her. In her current charcoal-gray pumps, they were the same height. She was five three on a good day. He'd always had a Napoleon complex. What was it about little men and overcompensation?

His brown eyes were flinty as he looked her up and down. Was *haughty* a word you could apply to a man? Outside of a nineteenth-century drawing room, that is? She shook her head. *Focus.*

"Let me repeat myself. Why are you in here, and

what are you doing in my files on the Hexaun case?" Blood thumped in her temples as her blood pressure surged.

"I told you. I got locked out of my computer and needed to check on some of the event reports for an early call." He smirked.

"Yeah, sure you did. What is going on?" She managed to keep her voice level. Something didn't add up here.

"You've always been dramatic. Fine, I'll tell you. You're off the case. It's mine now, and it will be a career maker for me. I just wanted to get an early start on it." Triumph permeated his smug tone.

"Wow. That's all it ever is for you, right? Making a name for yourself. Well, fine, take it. You know they're dirty. You know what's in those reports. How can you gloat? Be excited to represent them?" Had he always been completely amoral? She clenched her teeth, tamping down the urge to kick him in the shins.

"Don't be ridiculous. You've represented these clients and plenty of others just like them. It *is* your job. Remember? Don't worry about those reports. Or did you conveniently forget about attorney-client privilege?"

"You're right. I'm sick of these types of clients. All they care about is money." Just like him. He'd never cared about her, just used her to get closer to her father and onto the firm's partnership track.

"Not all of us were born with a silver spoon like you." A sneer marred his ordinary features. "You need to grow up. It's—"

"Grow up? Go to hell. They know their drug causes cancer, they've buried event reports, and there's email evidence. I'm briefing my father today and recommending the firm drop the case." She clasped her hands behind her, digging her fingernails into her palms.

"Drop it? Do you know how much money they pay us? There's no proof. You're just grasping at straws." His eyes widened.

"Who *are* you?" She threw up her hands in disgust. "Get out of my office. Now."

"Calm down." He backed out of her office and slammed the door.

She sank into her chair, closed her eyes, and gripped her desk with trembling hands. She inhaled three shaky breaths, willing her rapid pulse to regulate. What was he up to?

When she scanned her computer screen, the overflowing Trash Bin icon jumped out at her. She frowned and opened it. A few hundred Hexaun emails appeared, ready to be propelled off to cyberspace. If he'd actually emptied the trash, the incriminating correspondence would've disappeared. Her stomach clenched, and a bitter taste assaulted her throat. Not on her watch. She dragged and dropped them back into the client folder and then emailed the whole file to her personal email address. Unusual, yes, but her gut urged her to ensure records weren't expunged. Even though she was resigning, she would make sure her father received all the pertinent information. Lives were at stake.

The joyous little confrontation with Robert had started her juices flowing. It was eight a.m. Her father would be drinking his first cup of coffee at his desk. Time to face him.

Although the office was always precisely sixty-seven degrees, a trickle of sweat ran down Kelly's spine as she marched toward her father's corner office. Or trudged to the guillotine, as the case may be. She endeavored to keep her heartbeat steady and maintain her composure. Just as she had with Robert. Yeah, right.

She tapped on the heavy wooden door and strode into her father's office, her heels sinking into the plush carpet. Because Alistair Prescott III enjoyed looking down on people, his desk was elevated higher than the two uncomfortable chairs facing it. Actually, throne was a more appropriate term for the behemoth antique, one of his countless power-play tricks.

His distinguished silver eyebrows arched, and piercing onyx gaze bored into her. At sixty, he was severely handsome, with a sharp blade of a nose, slashing cheekbones, and a strong chin. He sipped his coffee—black, no sugar—and remained silent.

Always the master negotiator, he knew the rule: whoever speaks first loses. He'd employed the silent technique to great effect over the decades he'd amassed his legal empire.

She perched on the edge of the chair facing him. She smoothed back a tendril of hair, cleared her throat, and plunged in. "I'll just get to the point. Dad, as you know I've been dissatisfied with my role here for some time—"

"Dissatisfied?" He placed his china coffee cup onto a saucer and narrowed his gaze. "You're joking, right? You're on partnership track, you're set to take over the firm if you don't screw up, and you make an excellent salary and have a corner office."

"I'm aware. And you are aware it isn't what's important to me." She forced her voice to remain steady. "I've played the game for five years now, and I just can't do it anymore. I want to—"

"*Want?*" He pushed to his feet, slapped his palms on the desk, and glowered down at her. "Grow up. This isn't a game. This is real life. You are a Prescott, and this firm is the Prescott legacy. I handed you this opportunity, and I forbid you to leave." His skin flushed, and each word landed in the air like a slap.

Not so cool and controlled now, are you, Dad?

"You didn't *hand* me anything. My grades were exemplary, and my work is too. But that's not the point. This firm might be your life and your legacy, but it isn't mine." Her entire body trembled, but she stood her ground.

He glared at her but remained silent.

"I've felt this way for a while. I tried to do this for you, but I can't anymore. This Hexaun case is the nail in the proverbial coffin. They're committing fraud and worse, and Robert was in my office this morning, trying to delete emails. I won't be a part of it." A spurt of righteous anger stiffened her spine.

"Be careful what accusations you fling around. Hexaun is one of our biggest clients, and it is our duty to defend and protect them vigorously."

"Oh, so now that includes knowingly allowing them to tamper with evidence showing their magic drug will kill more people than it helps? Don't you care it causes cancer?" She'd never been close to her dad, but she'd respected his ethics. Had she misjudged him?

"Stop reacting like a woman and use your brain." His eyes chilled to shards of glass.

"Where's the moral code you swore to uphold? Does the money mean so much to you you'll look the other way?" Her father used to pride himself on his integrity. And the woman card? Really?

He sank back into his huge leather chair and sipped his coffee. Composed himself. "Kelly, usually your sense of fairness and justice is an asset. But there's no proof of anything illegal. You're jumping to conclusions. We cannot afford to offend or jeopardize our relationship with Hexaun. Robert is fully capable of handling it. So let it go."

"Hexaun is just one example." She inhaled deeply and pressed her hands against her churning belly. "Father, I'm giving you my two weeks' notice. I resign." Her exhale whooshed out.

"Resignation?" Surprise flickered behind his dark eyes. "Aren't you being a little melodramatic?"

"No, I'm not. I resign." She refused to offer justifications.

He stared at her as if she were an insect under a magnifying glass held by a seven-year-old boy ready to fry her in the noon sun.

"Do you need a vacation? Is that it? I can give you a week off to get yourself together." His gaze returned to his computer screen, dismissing her.

"Here's my formal resignation letter." Her hands trembled, but her voice was steady as she stood and placed it onto his desk, right under his aristocratic nose.

He glanced at the letter and flicked his gaze back to her. He tore it in two and pitched it into the trash bin under his desk.

"I refuse to accept it. Take the day off and come back tomorrow ready to act like a professional." He picked up his coffee.

"You're being ridiculous. I quit. I'll email another copy over to you and HR." A cleansing burst of fury supplanted fear in her heart. She turned to leave, determined not to expose her anger and heartbreak.

He slammed to his feet again and thumped the desk with his hand. "If you leave this firm, you leave this family." His voice was practically a whisper.

"What?" She angled back toward him, unable to trust her hearing.

"I will disown you. You will no longer be my daughter. You won't be welcome here or in my home." His face glowed beet red, his eyes narrowed, and he slapped the desk again. His controlled demeanor had evaporated.

"Are you serious? We aren't living in the middle of a gothic novel. This is just work. The firm will be fine without me." Her skin chilled, and a buzzing started in her ears.

"I am completely serious. You walk out of this door, and you are cut off."

"Dad…we already lost Peter—" A sob caught in her throat. So much for maintaining a stoic façade.

"Your brother chose his path, and you'll be dead to me as much as he is." Could his eyes be any colder? His expression more remote?

She hesitated, hugged her arms around her waist. How could he talk about Peter that way? His only son? Her only brother?

"I know you're angry now. I hope you change your mind." She walked toward the door, the humming in her ears escalating like an angry swarm of bees, her legs leaden. She would not allow him to witness her devastation.

"Get your belongings and be out of the office in fifteen minutes, or I'll send security to escort you out." Each word stabbed her in the back.

With chilled, numb fingers, she turned the brass doorknob and escaped from his icy verbal assault. She pulled the door closed behind her with a silent click and stared sightlessly into the now-bustling cubicles that comprised the main floor. She pivoted toward her soon-to-be-former office and took the first few uncertain steps toward her future.

Chapter 5

Christian accelerated his pace, despite the screaming of his calf muscles and the burning in his lungs. Failing to finish the ten-mile run was not an option. Axl Rose screeched in his ear to take him down to Paradise City. Right now, Paradise City would be his Jacuzzi and an ice-cold beer. Unfortunately, he was on the final loop, and the steamy hot tub and cold beverage may as well have been a million miles away.

Part of his brain urged him to slow to a walk, but his legs continued to propel him up the steep road winding through the Laguna hills. The pain served to drown out the memories haunting him, but at this rate, his lungs would probably explode before he finished his workout.

His phone buzzed and interrupted the heavy metal music pumping through his earbuds. Damn it, what now? He glanced down at the iPhone screen, and Nick's name flashed. He hadn't seen Nick as frequently since his buddy got married, so it was a good excuse to stop, right? He'd go throw around some dumbbells later and make up for the missed miles.

"Hey." He exhaled the syllable.

"Running again? You sound like a braying donkey." Nick's tone was dry, as usual.

"Ha ha. Some of us have to stay in shape." He struggled to moderate his breathing, lengthening his inhales and exhales. Screw it. He stopped and put his hands on his thighs and bent forward to cool down.

"Save some energy—I've got a favor if you've got a few hours."

"I'm not building anything for you, so just forget it." Nick was an architect and had on more than one occasion suckered him into helping on the construction end of a few projects. Not that he minded physical labor, but...

"No, no. I just need some of your big manly muscles to help move some boxes. A few hours, tops."

He snorted. Nick was such a dick. "I'm oiling up those manly muscles for a Studs of Laguna photo shoot today, so not sure if I can spare time to lift a finger."

Nick guffawed. "Damn, man, I can't unsee that visual. Seriously, I just need a little help. You remember Sophie's best friend, Kelly?"

"Yeah." Shit. Since he'd seen her last week, she'd starred in a few of his daydreams, sporting her librarian glasses, blood-red stilettos, and nothing else.

"Well, she's renting our cottage. It's furnished, so she's just got clothes and boxes. Sophie asked me to help, but I can't get out of a last-minute meeting. I figured I'd volunteer you."

"This afternoon?" He struggled to create an excuse, but his brain was as fried as his legs. "I'm really busy right—"

"C'mon. Just an hour or two? It'd really help me out, help her out."

"Fine. When?" Damn it.

"She's actually on her way up right now. It was all kind of last minute. Any way you could head over now?"

He was going to kill Nick when he saw him next. "I'm out for my run and need to go home and shower." Didn't he?

"Nah, don't shower. You'll just get sweaty again. Where are you?"

Christian ran his tongue around his teeth. By some stroke of fate, he was about four blocks from Nick's house and the cottage on the lower part of his property. Shit.

"I'm actually pretty close. I'll go over now." What was he afraid of? He'd faced combat on four separate tours in Iraq and Afghanistan; he could act nonchalant around a pretty woman.

"I owe you. We'll have you over for dinner. Sophie makes an amazing lasagna."

His stomach grumbled, reminding him he'd only had a protein shake for breakfast and he loved lasagna. His grandmother's recipe was the best he'd ever had, but how could he turn down a home-cooked meal? Hell, he didn't have anything better to do until going into Vines tonight. He could handle seeing Kelly—valiant soldier that he was.

"I'm headed over now. Warning you I'm ripe." He was soaked with sweat and pretty positive he reeked like a wet dog.

"Thanks again, dude. Oh, by the way, Kelly's single." Nick hung up without waiting for a reply.

Single? Moving to Laguna? And working for Peaceful Warrior. Complicated. Shaking his head, he half jogged the few blocks to Nick's property. As he walked up the curved driveway, an engine rattled behind him. He turned to see Kelly behind the wheel of what must have been an antique moving truck. He

35

waved, and she returned the gesture, but even from a distance he saw her furrowed brow. Nick obviously hadn't informed her he was sending a replacement.

****

Kelly steered the hunk of junk the gum-snapping moving company employee had foisted on her up the driveway. Last-minute reservations meant slim pickings in the rental truck world. She'd made it up to Laguna by a prayer and a miracle. Her shoulders softened, and her lips curved up. She'd arrived.

Oh my. Oh my. *Oh my.*

A man with a powerful, broad shouldered, tapered V-back and perfect ass was motoring up the drive. She rubbed her eyes, honed her gaze, and checked to ensure she wasn't hallucinating. The Greek god's drenched white tank top clung to his bronzed sinewy back—he was ripped—and his army-green running shorts showcased long, sculpted legs sprinkled with dark hair.

Sophie had mentioned Nick was planning on helping to move any heavy stuff into the house, but this stud wasn't her best friend's husband. This physique belonged to Christian Wolfe. He'd been handsome in street clothes, but halfway unclothed, he was mouthwatering.

She parked the heap of metal in front of the cottage and cleared her throat. Something about him caused her cheeks to warm and her nerves to kick in. *Don't act like a dork. Don't drool.* She pried open the truck's rusty door and climbed out.

"Hey, Christian, what are you doing here?" And where was Sophie? Nick?

"Hi, Kelly. Nick recruited me. Nice truck by the way." His eyes were concealed behind mirrored aviators. Five-o'clock shadow tempted her to brush her fingers over his square jaw.

"Only the finest. I'm lucky I made it up here." She laughed. Okay, so maybe he had a sense of humor under the stoic exterior. "Umm, where's Nick? And Sophie should be here." Heat rose up the back of her neck. Was he sporting an eight-pack under his damp tank top? *Do not take a flying leap and tackle him to the ground and cover his sculpted torso with kisses.*

"No, something came up, so here I am. Let's do this." Zero expression on his face.

"Thanks. Okay, I think the cottage is unlocked. Here's the key for the truck padlock. I'll prop open the front door, and we'll knock this out." She could play it cool. Right?

He grunted, grabbed the key, and headed toward the back of the truck. His muscular arm brushed her shoulder, and they both jolted at the connection. Her scalp tingled, and the little hairs on the back of her neck lifted.

The truck door groaned open immediately. Apparently, Mr. Strong and Silent was serious about getting started. Fine, she'd made a career of presenting an all-business façade. She could squash her physical attraction to him.

She wiped her damp palms on her shorts, grabbed the bags of groceries she'd bought at her new local supermarket, and headed into her new home. She crammed the food in the refrigerator, planning to organize it later. She paused to admire the airy, sun-filled living room Nick's interior designer sister, Alyssa, had created. Thank goodness she'd chosen to stow most of her belongings in storage.

Even without her furniture, she'd crammed the moving truck with her favorite paintings and pictures, too many boxes of books to count—thank goodness Christian had the brawn to lug them all in—and all her clothes. And shoes.

"Where do you want the boxes of bricks?" His raspy voice sounded from behind her.

She turned, and he was framed in the doorway, his defined biceps bulging with two hefty book cartons stacked under his chin. He quirked a dark brow. He'd pushed the sunglasses back onto his thick deep brown hair, and his eyes glowed a sparkling mossy green. A different color from the last time she saw them. Her lips parted, and her mind blanked.

"Anytime. They only weigh about fifty pounds." Not a hint of a smile.

"Sorry, sorry. How about against the far wall in the living room, under the window? Actually, all the book boxes can go there. Wardrobe boxes in the bedroom. Obviously." Her cheeks heated when she said bedroom. Geez, what was wrong with her? He was just really, *really* hot.

He crossed the polished hardwood floor, set the boxes down under the enormous picture window, and headed back to the truck without a word.

She huffed out a breath and shook her head. *Pull it together, Prescott. Pull it together.* She returned to the truck, and he passed her, carting the heavy cartons as if they contained feather pillows instead of the makings of a public library. Impressive.

They worked in silence. She'd caught a whiff of his sweaty, masculine scent. Admired his powerful catlike stride. Each time they passed each other through the doorway, he managed to avoid touching her again. Was he making a concerted effort not to?

Who could blame him? Maybe she smelled a little ripe. After all, her rented moving truck didn't have air conditioning and her ancient T-shirt usually reserved for cleaning day clung to her. She resisted the urge to sniff herself. Damp tendrils from her messy topknot itched the back of her neck.

Earlier this morning, she'd been eager to embark on her new life, so getting on the road was the priority. If she'd known the hottest guy she'd ever seen would be there, perhaps she'd have showered before high-tailing it out of Solana Beach. Not that he appeared to notice.

Circling toward the back of the truck, she stopped to admire the view. Christian was crouched down in the far end of the truck with his back turned. He had the cutest butt she'd ever seen. She wasn't ogling. No, she was simply appreciating beauty, right?

He rose and turned toward her, dusting off his hands. "That's everything, right?"

"Um, yeah. Thanks so much." She swallowed. "Can I get you anything to drink?" Somehow her usually talkative brain was operating in slow motion today. Must be the move. Sure, it was the move.

"I've gotta run." He vaulted gracefully out of the truck and landed within inches of her.

Heat shot down her spine as their gaze remained locked, his shimmering tiger eyes unreadable. Without a word, he turned and jogged down the driveway. As he receded from view, she released the breath she'd been holding.

****

Kelly slammed the heavy moving-truck door shut and secured the lock. Another stage complete. She dusted off her hands and headed inside. Now to unpack, organize, and put her stamp on her new home.

As she walked in the door, Sophie called.

"Hey, what happened to you?"

"I'm so sorry. I got tied up. I'm heading down now. Do you want to go grab some lunch?"

"I actually hit the grocery store on the way up. I've got stuff for sandwiches if you're cool with turkey on wheat?" And she'd need an industrial-strength shower to be seen in public anytime soon.

"Perfect. Is Nick still there?" Sophie asked.

"Nick didn't show up—something about an urgent meeting. He sent Christian instead. He just left." All six-foot something of enigmatic male.

"Hold that thought. I'll be right there. Walking down the hill." Nick and Sophie lived in the main house, only a short distance from the cottage.

Kelly headed to the refrigerator and pulled out the bread, oven-roasted turkey breast, arugula, and yellow mustard. Both she and Sophie enjoyed a simple sandwich for lunch.

"I'm so happy you're here. Was it fun watching the big strong man carry heavy boxes?" Sophie pursed her lips as she entered the cottage.

"Best view I've had in a long time. He is *hot*. He'd been running and was all tall, dark, and sweaty. And definitely silent. What's his deal?" Was he that way with everyone or just her?

"He's been single since I've known him. No girlfriend I know of. He's never brought a date to any of our parties or even to the wedding." Sophie leaned against the granite countertop.

"Please tell me he isn't another Player of Laguna like Nick and Brandt were." She didn't have the energy for anything complicated.

"I don't think so. He's kind of mysterious. You should ask him out." Sophie smiled mischievously as she plopped onto a barstool.

"What? You're kidding, right? I'm not asking him out. He can ask me out." Call her old-fashioned, but she wanted to be pursued, and she wouldn't run from Christian Wolfe.

Sophie laughed. "I get it. Well, I wouldn't be a good best friend if I didn't offer to assist in this situation, would I? I'll have a dinner party. You'll be able to hang out with him in an environment you'll both be comfortable in. We'll invite Alyssa and Brandt too." She rubbed her hands together and grinned.

"Ha ha, it'll be perfect. As long as he doesn't suspect a setup." Kelly smiled as she sliced the sandwich into two symmetrical triangles and set it in front of Sophie. She turned back to make her own.

"Well, he sure checked you out the first time you visited, remember? I was so annoyed you'd invited Nick out with us, and when we walked in, you two made googly eyes."

"I will never speak to you again if you bring up the googly eyes ever again." She swallowed a giggle. "But why not?"

Sophie clapped her hands together. "How perfect would it be if you two ended up together? Then we can become old married ladies together."

"Whoa! Don't go marrying me off just yet. I want to focus on this new job and maybe have some fun with

Laguna's resident Heathcliff." She paused and took a bite of her sandwich.

"Do you want to return the truck and get your car today or tomorrow? I can do either."

"Tomorrow is fine. I want to settle in today." Until she'd unpacked everything, she wouldn't be able to completely relax.

"Anything from your parents?" Sophie asked gently.

The turkey sandwich turned to dust in her throat, and her stomach clenched. "Not a word. I think my dad was serious about disowning me. Medieval, right? And you know my mom. Pop a tranquilizer and head out to the pool and read magazines." They were a pair of cold fish.

Sophie set down her lunch and hugged her. "Hey, we can't choose our parents—you always pointed that out to me. You're an amazing woman despite them, and don't you forget it."

Sophie's comforting words warmed her heart. Her best friend's mom was a piece of work, a brittle French woman who'd never recovered from Sophie's dad abandoning them. Despite not having nurturing parents, they'd each blossomed and excelled. They weren't the products of their environment

"Okay, enough of being maudlin. Let's unpack some boxes. After we get through a few, it's probably time for happy hour." Kelly smiled in anticipation of creating her new sanctuary, her impeccably organized, streamlined, ready-to-change-the-world sanctuary.

Chapter 6

Christian's phone pinged. He glanced at the screen. Nick was texting to invite him over tomorrow night for the promised lasagna dinner. Payment for lugging what felt like fifty boxes of bricks into Kelly's new home.

What else did he have to do? It wasn't as if he had a wild social life. Hell, for the close to two years he'd been back in the States, he'd spent the spare time when he wasn't working out with his nose buried in a book. He placed the dog-eared copy of *The Sun Also Rises* onto the glass-top coffee table.

Hemingway was his favorite author. He understood the aftermath of war, the scars not visible to the naked eye. Books had been one of his biggest comforts in Iraq, where sleep had often eluded him. They provided an escape from the nightmares that haunted him when he could actually drift off. Yeah, people thought he looked the same as he had before the Middle East, but appearances were deceiving.

He answered the text, levered off the sofa, and strolled over to peruse his wine selection. Definitely an advantage of owning the wine bar. Who knew he'd love the wine business so much? Probably his maternal grandmother's influence combined with the Italian blood coursing through his veins. In less than two years, he'd managed to create a spot popular with both connoisseurs and casual clientele alike.

Adjusting to being an entrepreneur after a decade in the military wasn't easy, but he loved Vines and loved being back in Southern California. He'd attended San Diego State University on a ROTC scholarship and majored in business because he figured one day he'd need to run his own gig. After officer training school in Fort Benning, Georgia, he'd progressed through Airborne and then Ranger School, finishing as a second lieutenant, paratrooper, and ranger.

At one point, he'd led a twelve-man A-Team and advised a hundred-man Iraqi commando unit. Sometimes he missed the camaraderie with his Special Forces buddies, both American and Iraqi.

Did he want to go back to the Middle East?

Hell no.

Did he want to be responsible for a platoon of soldiers again and feel the weight of the world on his shoulders when tragedy struck?

Hell no, sir.

Could he ever release the guilt plaguing him over all the men who'd trusted him, respected him, and had died or been maimed carrying out his orders? Especially Davidson.

Doubtful.

Nick Morgan was one of the few friends he'd stayed in touch with who wasn't connected to the military. He could count on him, although he didn't see him as often now he'd gotten married. And he couldn't deny his wife's beautiful best friend intrigued him.

What were the odds he was finally considering getting some assistance for his nightmares and panic attacks and Kelly was going to be working at the only local veteran organization? It wasn't as if Laguna was a big city with tons of different resources from which to choose. Nope, just Peaceful Warrior.

****

Kelly poked her head into the powder room at Nick and Sophie's house and checked her pale pink lipstick for the twentieth time. She turned her head side to side, squinting to analyze if the perfect mermaid waves she'd spent an hour to create hadn't devolved into a frizzy mop. She wasn't a neurotic mess, not at all. Her heart was racing, and her pupils were a little dilated. Christian hadn't even arrived yet.

"You look like a gorgeous tawny lioness, as usual." Alyssa's face popped up behind her in the mirror.

Talk about stunning: Alyssa was five ten and willowy. She could be a supermodel. If she weren't so funny and kind, she'd be easy to envy.

Kelly turned, and Nick's younger sister enveloped her in a hug. She hadn't seen Alyssa in ages. Last time they'd been together, they'd shared a girls' night with Sophie, complete with ratty sweats, vats of wine, and enough chocolate to solve anything. Both she and Alyssa had fought with their respective guys, but Brandt and Alyssa had reconciled and were now engaged.

"Everything okay? Sophie filled me in on what happened. I'm thrilled you're moving to Laguna, but sorry to hear about how it all went down." Alyssa's smooth brow creased.

"I'm fine. Kind of a whirlwind, but fine. Are you sure I look okay?" She'd mastered compartmentalizing her dysfunctional relationship with her charming father, but for some reason seeing Christian tonight rattled her. Why was she so nervous?

45

She glanced in the mirror again and shifted the neckline of her favorite white T-shirt two centimeters to the left. Her beachy ensemble and metallic wedge slides would have to suffice as armor against the flutter in her belly.

"Umm, yeah. Christian won't know what hit him." Alyssa laughed.

Did everyone know it was a setup? "I'm not trying to impress—"

"Don't worry. Sophie told me, but the guys don't have a clue. It's normal we'd all spend time together. Christian and Nick were friends growing up, although he was gone so long in the military I didn't see him much. He's a good guy." Alyssa patted her shoulder.

They headed into the enormous kitchen where Sophie, Nick, Brandt, and Christian were already gathered. The three men were a study in contrasts. Nick was a golden-haired god, a talented architect, and smitten with his lovely wife. Brandt looked like a laid-back gorgeous surfer dude, when in reality he was a self-made millionaire with a heart of gold and a tragic past. She could appreciate how handsome both her friends' guys were, but neither caused her heart rate to spike or her mouth to grow parched. Only Mr. Tall, Dark, and Stoic affected her.

Christian looked up when they entered. He had three bottles of red wine lined up on the kitchen island. Kelly's cheeks warmed—he hadn't seen her fussing in the powder room, had he?

Their gazes locked, and he quickly shifted his focus to Alyssa and grinned. Had she noticed the way his eyes crinkled at the corners when he smiled? Too bad the devastating smile wasn't directed at her.

"Everyone's here. Awesome. Okay, guys." Sophie took charge. "Christian, you open a bottle of wine. Nick, grab the hors d'oeuvres out of the fridge. Brandt, get the napkins and plates, and let's head into the living room. I've got a lasagna in the oven, so let's get started on these."

"Anything I can do to help?" Kelly smiled. Seeing her best friend happy and in her element warmed her heart.

"Nope, dinner's in your honor tonight. A welcome to Laguna. Just grab your glass of wine."

"Hey, I thought this dinner was for me breaking my back carrying in all those boxes of cinder blocks?" Christian paused in the middle of uncorking a bottle of red. Was that a streak of sarcasm? Another glimpse of a sense of humor? Maybe he wasn't the stereotypical strong and silent type after all.

"We'll make it a combo celebration. You stepping in at the last minute helped so much, and I know Kelly's really appreciative. Right, Kelly?" Sophie strolled toward the living room without waiting for an answer.

Talk about awkward pauses.

Kelly hesitated, unsure if she should offer to help carry the wine. Or offer to give him a back massage as a thank-you? A flashback to his gleaming tanned skin in a soaked white tank top hit her. She smoothed a strand of hair behind her ear and cleared her throat. *Get a grip, girl. He's a person, not a movie star.* Although he certainly could be.

"So how many boxes did you unpack?" Christian headed toward her, a wine bottle in each hand.

"All of them." She fell into step beside him. Who

would've thought he'd be the one initiating conversation?

"Are you kidding me?" He halted midstride and looked at her, his mossy-green eyes wide.

"Um, no, I like to be organized." She shrugged with a small smile. Some people called it "compulsive." She chose to call it "ruthlessly organized." Ha.

"That's what you call it?" He smirked.

"That's my story, and I'm sticking to it." Were they flirting? The butterflies circling in her tummy certainly believed it.

"Okay, then I won't bill you for the moving services after all." Wow, with even a half smile, his entire face lit up.

In the living room, he placed one bottle onto the coffee table and began filling everyone's glasses. Sophie and Nick snuggled on one end of the L-shaped sofa, and Brandt nuzzled Alyssa's neck on the other end. They'd left the love seat open for Christian and Kelly. She shot Sophie a dirty look. Could they at least *try* not to be so obvious?

Kelly accepted the glass of garnet red cabernet sauvignon from him and perched on the edge of the love seat. Christian joined her, the cushions sinking under his weight. His strong thigh brushed against hers, searing her through her jeans. His leg was about twice the size of hers and solid as steel.

Perspiration dampened her T-shirt between her shoulder blades. Was it getting warm in the room? She looked around, but the two happy couples appeared oblivious.

She leaned forward to select one of the tasty looking miniature quiches at the same time as Christian, and their shoulders bumped. The fine hairs on her arms jumped to attention as awareness sparked down her spine. He smelled like fresh laundry, an aroma she'd always found appealing. She restrained the rather-urgent urge to lean in closer and sniff him.

She dared a sidelong glance. At close range, his green eyes were gilded with amber and gold and surrounded by thick black lashes. His pupils flared, and his firm lips parted. Okay, she wasn't the only hot-and-bothered person on this love seat. Maybe this setup masquerading as a casual get-together was a good idea.

She maintained eye contact and nibbled on a morsel of quiche. She flicked a crumb off her lip and prayed she looked sexy instead of like a slob. Christian snapped into a ramrod straight position and inhaled sharply. Her breath caught, and everything else faded into the background. Awareness simmered in the air.

Bailey, Nick and Sophie's horse of a dog, galloped into the room, skidded to a halt, and smacked into Kelly's legs. At the impact, she braced one hand against Christian's powerful thigh and lifted her wineglass to the side to prevent unwanted red polka dots from decorating her white ensemble.

"Bailey!" Nick snapped, and the mutt plopped her butt down with a sheepish grin, her pink tongue lolling.

Kelly shifted back to her side of the love seat and inhaled a huge sip of her wine and exhaled slowly.

"You okay, guys? You know Bailey—she's just so darned big she slams into everything without trying." Sophie laughed.

"Bailey's actually Cupid in disguise." Alyssa gestured with her wineglass toward Christian. "Have you heard the story?"

He shook his head but remained silent.

"So when Sophie first rented the cottage, she couldn't find the keys." Alyssa apparently wasn't deterred by his impassive reaction. "She dumped her whole purse on the porch and was pawing through to find them. Bailey bounded up and knocked her down. When Nick helped her up, sparks flew and it was love at first fall." Alyssa pursed her lips and made kissy sounds.

"You just love to tease them, don't you?" Kelly scratched Bailey's floppy black ears.

"Yes, I do." Alyssa laughed and snuggled in closer to Brandt. "Do you think she was trying to play Cupid with you two?"

Kelly's cheeks warmed, and she glared at Alyssa. Time to change the subject. What if he suspected they'd discussed setting them up?

An uncomfortable silence hung in the air, and then Christian reached one sinewy arm over to give Bailey another scratch. Bailey's tail started thumping. Kelly inhaled when the crisp dark hairs on his tanned arms brushed against her. His hands were large, square palmed, and powerful. The heat in her cheeks traveled south, and she prayed the couch didn't burst into flames.

"Bailey, come here." Sophie laughed as she directed the dog to lie down. "She'll somehow manage to sneak something off your plate if you aren't careful. She's shameless."

Bailey wasn't the only shameless female in the room. If she scooted over one inch closer to Christian, they'd be connected from armpit to ankle. She gripped the wineglass to avoid the temptation to brush her fingers along his chiseled chest. Kelly settled back and sipped her delicious wine and fought to regulate her accelerated heartbeat.

"Oh, I forgot. Coolest thing ever. I've started reviewing some of the emails for Peaceful Warrior and—" Kelly began, desperate to shift her focus to anything but her hyperawareness of his proximity.

"You aren't starting for another week. Why are you already working?" Sophie shook her head.

She held up a hand. "I know, I know. But, well, I had some time, and I figured why not. Anyway, I think I'm going to implement a new program. There's a group called Pups-4-Vets who rescues dogs from animal shelters and rescue groups. The trainers test their temperaments, and if the dogs pass, they train them to be service animals for returning veterans. Isn't that cool?"

"Amazing. I love that they aren't breeding more dogs but giving these discarded babies a second chance," Sophie said. As if on cue, her cat, Zack, materialized on the back of the couch.

"It sounds awesome. So for disabled vets in wheelchairs and stuff?" Nick nodded. "Christian, you heard of this?"

"Sure." His voice was neutral.

"Well, I like that the dogs aren't just for physical disabilities, but really help those with posttraumatic stress and other psychiatric issues too." Kelly said. The invisible wounds could be the deepest.

Christian subtly shifted away from her. Without him pressed against her body, her overheated skin chilled immediately.

"Don't you have some of your former guys dealing

with PTS?" Brandt said.

"Sure." Christian's face was once again carved from granite, and no hint of humor remained. He stood, managing to avoid brushing against her. He plucked one of the empty wine bottles off the table and strode back toward the kitchen.

What was up?

****

Christian struggled to play it cool and eased off the sofa. He needed air, but the kitchen would at least provide him space. Damn it, one mention of posttraumatic stress and he'd freaked out. One innocuous discussion and all he could see was Private Roger Davidson's arm blown to smithereens, as if it were yesterday.

Sitting next to Kelly had been an exquisite torture. Warm and slightly exotic, her sweet cinnamon scent tempted him to kiss her. Each brush of her silky skin against him lured him to touch her. The laughter dancing in her unusual golden eyes mesmerized him.

He wasn't an idiot. He'd noticed they'd left the love seat for them. Attached couples always wanted to play matchmaker, and he was sure it wasn't an accident. He didn't care. She was beautiful and smart, and sparks flew whenever he saw her. He was open to dating her, as long as it remained casual.

He'd been focused on getting his body under control. Hell, he hadn't had sex in over a year, and every fiber of his being was on high alert. Then Kelly brought up the service dogs for Peaceful Warrior. Talk about a way to kill the mood.

He placed the empty bottle into the recycle bin and braced his hands on the granite countertop. He closed his eyes and forced himself to breathe. Damn it, he couldn't talk about wounded veterans. His friends couldn't see his scars, but they lurked beneath the surface and he wouldn't allow them to show. Not now, maybe not ever.

Why'd she have to take a job there of all places?

No more Kelly Prescott. No more fantasizing about her damn red stilettos and full lips. The minute she discovered how screwed up he was, her interest would morph into viewing him as another charity case. He wouldn't be anybody's project.

"Time for dinner," Sophie piped up from behind him. "Christian, will you herd everybody over to the dining room table, and I'll bring out the lasagna."

"Sure, of course. What I do best." He forced a smile.

"Dinner. Now," he yelled over his shoulder. When everyone trooped to the enormous table, he refused to glance at Kelly.

She sat directly across from him, but he managed to look everywhere except at her. Instead, he directed the conversation to surfing and the guys jumped right on it. Any remorse at ignoring her was buried. It was safer that way.

After Sophie carted out an enormous apple pie, courtesy of Alyssa "the Baking Angel," he excused himself on the pretext of meeting a buddy for an early morning run.

Was he officially a coward? Sure. But in this case it was justified. No sense in giving Kelly the impression they'd become the next happy couple in Laguna. Not in the cards.

Chapter 7

Kelly wiped the sweat from her brow, leaned back in her comfortable office chair, and surveyed the considerable progress she'd achieved in her broom closet of a new office. After burrowing like a mole through stacks of banker boxes and mountains of manila folders, she'd unearthed the scarred relic that would serve as her desk. And the surprisingly shiny new computer buried under heaps of papers.

Eager to begin her new career, she'd arrived bright and early Monday morning. She'd finally be the boss and head of the department. No matter the department consisted of one employee, herself. Petty detail.

Although the office was casual, she'd wanted—no, needed—to feel confident. Professional clothes provided armor, and if she looked the part, she'd fulfill it, as she had for five years in her dad's firm. She wore gray trousers and a white button-down blouse with her signature stilettos, this time in peacock blue. Unfortunately, one of her four-inch heels had caught on some unidentifiable object amidst the clutter, and she'd face-planted two steps into the room. At least nobody was in her office to hear her curse, so she didn't have to admit her clumsiness to anyone. If nobody saw you trip in the forest, it didn't actually happen, right?

She'd recovered her dignity and vowed to establish order in the cyclone of a room mere seconds before

Susan, her secretary and Mr. Williams's wife, popped her head in the door. The "Old Bird" nickname didn't fit at all. Susan was an attractive, slender blonde who seemed friendly and sharp.

When asked about the disaster area of an office, Susan shrugged. "It's a nonprofit." She had, however, begun researching storage spaces for the mountain of boxes that needed to be moved off-site. Progress.

Satisfied she could at least enter and exit the room and sit at her desk without the threat of gasping out her last breath beneath a pile of wayward boxes, Kelly plucked a fresh yellow legal pad from her camel-colored leather briefcase. She pulled up the list of programs offered by Peaceful Warrior and uncapped a microfine blue rollerball pen. Time to review her to-do list prior to her eleven o'clock meeting with her new boss.

She'd reviewed the legal folders and actual claims at play. The list was longer than she'd anticipated. Several of the vets who were applying for legal aid appeared to be struggling with the basics of survival. Damn it, they deserved better treatment after sacrificing for the country.

"Ms. Prescott, are you ready to meet?" Mr. Williams's gruff voice questioned from the doorway.

"Of course. Should we meet here, or would you prefer I come to your office?"

He approached and dropped down onto one of the chairs facing her now-clean desk. "I can actually breathe in here, so let's stay here. Impressive cleanup by the way." He nodded in approval.

"Thanks, I operate better when everything is in its place. Let's begin by reviewing the current lawsuits, then move on to the various programs in play and the ones we're looking to add, and whatever else you'd like me to focus on in my first thirty days." She leaned forward in her seat.

"Okay. And please call me Bill. No need to be formal."

"Bill Williams?" She would *not* laugh.

"Yeah, my parents were real creative. William Williams." He grinned. "Anyway, in the past an outside law firm handled our cases. Set up a meeting with them to review everything and make sure nothing slips through the cracks during the transition." He paused and gazed down at the notebook in his lap.

"I've scheduled an appointment for tomorrow morning with Bob Atchison. I was disheartened to see all the cases for eviction, wrongful termination, personal injury, and various misdemeanors. Other than that, is there anything in particular I should know before meeting him?" *Like are they competent attorneys, were we on the back burner because we didn't pay full rates, did they win them all or...* A million questions flitted through her brain.

"We've got several medical cases against both the Department of Veteran Affairs for disability and a few filed under the Federal Tort Claim Act. Any questions about which ones are pursued in which forum?"

"It's my understanding if a VA doctor or other employee of the VA injures a person, two options exist. When an employee of the VA acts negligently and causes an injury, the preferred venue is in federal court. If an injury occurs resulting from a VA hospital, outpatient clinic, medical exam, or surgery, claims are more limited under Section 1151. Correct?" She sounded like a law school student proudly reciting code. Geez. Veterans Affairs, or the VA, had different rules than the state and federal jurisdictions she was accustomed to working in.

"Exactly. Atchison's firm handled many of our cases pro bono or for a limited fee, and we might not have been top priority. Just make sure each one is being handled thoroughly." He frowned at her and scrunched his brow.

"Of course. Don't worry." She injected a note of false confidence into her tone. Now wasn't the time to wonder if she'd bitten off more than she could chew. She was smart. She could do this. If she could succeed in the cutthroat world of corporate litigation for five years, she could succeed at anything.

They discussed a few more specific files, and once Kelly believed they'd covered the top priorities, she steered the discussion toward the current programs offered by Peaceful Warrior.

"Before we add new programs, can we review what's working with the current ones?" She shrugged. "What should we keep, and what needs to be tossed?"

"We've got a fairly full schedule and excellent relationships in the Laguna community. We're in good shape with the current partners. I'd say it's why we've had such success with our members. Tell me your ideas for new alliances." He gestured with his ballpoint pen and flipped over a new sheet on his yellow legal pad.

"It's wonderful you've established so many strong partnerships. So you like dogs, right?" Why not dive right into her pet project?

"Dogs?" His eyebrows flew up. "Sure, Susan and I have a min pin. Vito's the best."

"Vito?" She struggled not to laugh at the pride in his voice.

"Best guard dog you'll ever meet. All twelve pounds of him. What about you?" A smile creased his leathery face and warmed his dark eyes.

"I had Homer, a chocolate Lab, when I was a child, but then law school started and then came the partnership track at the law firm. It wouldn't have been fair to a dog to keep it cooped up all day." She smiled at the memory of the fur ball that had provided so much love and comfort in her sterile childhood life. She shook her head. Now was definitely not the time to reminisce.

"Anyway, I've learned of an amazing organization called Pups-4-Vets. They save dogs from shelters and animal-rescue groups and test them to be therapy dogs. If the dogs have the proper temperament, they adopt them, spend a year training them, and then give them to veterans with a variety of needs from physical to mental and emotional issues." Her heart warmed at the wonderful work the group did.

"Really? I know service dogs can make a huge difference in these vets' lives. Is it expensive, though?"

"That's the beauty of it. It's a nonprofit, and they find donors who help fund the training and adoption fees. I've scheduled an appointment for Saturday morning to go out and meet the director. And see the dogs." She was giddy with anticipation.

"Already? You move fast. And they're interested in working with us?" His eyes widened.

"Definitely. They are a national organization, and their dogs are placed all over the country. But they're interested in aligning themselves with a local group.

They're located about an hour away in Menifee, so it benefits us."

"Go for it. If you think it's a fit, go ahead and sign us up." He nodded and glanced down at his notepad. "I've got to get back to my desk now. Do you have anything else?"

"Not right now. I think I've got plenty to dig into." She pushed her glasses back up onto the bridge of her nose.

"Good. We'll debrief tomorrow after your meeting with outside counsel." He rose and headed toward the door. "I think you're going to be a great asset, Kelly," he called over his shoulder.

When he exited, she heaved a sigh of relief and sank back into her chair. She slid her glasses off her nose and massaged her temples. All things considered, the meeting had gone extremely well. She liked the new role: what a complete shift from her law firm position.

Pushing her glasses back onto her nose, she located the file labeled "Meditation." A local yoga-and-meditation teacher came once a week and taught mantra meditation in the large room they had for various types of meetings and programs. Perfect. No more excuses.

She'd always been fascinated by the research behind meditation, which found that learning to direct your thoughts could help you alleviate a variety of ailments. And it could be an excellent way for her to meet some of the regular vets who were part of the center.

She clicked over to the registration for tonight's session—way to start her first day of work—and choked on the sip of coffee she'd just taken. Christian Wolfe's name was at the top of the list. He had an asterisk by his name, which signified it was his first time.

Was that why he'd been outside Peaceful Warrior before her interview? He'd frozen her out after she mentioned the service dogs, so she didn't anticipate him confiding in her.

She paused and removed her glasses again, gazing off through the tiny window she'd unearthed during her cleaning frenzy. All she could see was the hint of green leaves and tree bark. She squinted. Was that a sliver of ocean? Not exactly the floor-to-ceiling windows she'd enjoyed at the Prescott Firm, but she'd take it. She didn't miss her old life a single bit.

Did Christian miss the camaraderie of fellow military? He'd retired early and returned to Laguna, so who knew? He'd had a distinguished career and probably wouldn't want to exhibit any vulnerability. What would he do when he saw her? Would he run away, as he'd done from Sophie's dinner?

Was he coming because of her? Was he interested after all?

Her belly tightened, and she squashed the dangerous line of thinking. He couldn't know she was planning to attend the meditation or any other program. If he had even thought about her at all.

If they saw each other tonight, maybe it was fate stepping in.

Chapter 8

Christian clicked off the ignition of his Jeep and closed his eyes. *Just go inside. What do you have to lose?*

Taking a deep breath, he stepped out of the car and marched to the Peaceful Warrior entrance. Unlike last time he'd been there, this time he'd actually cross the threshold. No more avoidance. Going to a meditation group wasn't a sign of weakness. Hell, all the professional athletes meditated before games, and nobody criticized them. And didn't Bill Gates swear by it?

No more second-guessing. He yanked open the door and entered the building. The lobby was well lit and painted a soft yellow. Although the popcorn ceilings were low and the building obviously wasn't new, it smelled like the old-fashion pine-scented cleaner his mom had used. A meditation flyer, mounted on a large, bright green sign with a white arrow, directed him to the end of the long hallway.

Ahead of him, a handful of people toting cushions and blankets chatted in muted tones. Shit, was he supposed to bring a pillow? Why didn't anyone tell him? His step hitched, but he forced himself to continue. He hated being unprepared.

He passed a few doors, one marked simply "Offices," and he increased his pace. Would Kelly be in there this late? He couldn't risk seeing her tonight. He was trying to calm his nervous system, not ratchet it up through the roof.

Finally, he entered the open door. He scanned the space and breathed a sigh of relief when he spotted the stack of plump cushions against one sky-blue wall. He headed over, selected a bolster, and sat at the far side of the large square room.

Of the dozen or so other people already gathered, nobody paid attention to him. The air didn't reek of patchouli or sandalwood, which was a good sign. Okay, this might work out.

A petite woman with sparkling white hair and a warm smile approached and crouched in front of him. "Hi there. I'm Pamela, the instructor. Welcome." She offered her narrow hand, and he shook it, appreciating her firm grip.

"Hi, I'm Christian."

"It's your first time here, right?" When he nodded, her smile deepened. "Do you have a meditation practice now?"

"Nope. I'm trying something new." And am hoping it will solve every single excruciating headache, bone-chilling, sweat-inducing nightmare, and overall sense of survivor's guilt. No pressure, though.

"Wonderful. Be patient with yourself. It can take several sessions to find your groove. We'll get started in a few minutes." She patted his leg and moved to the other side of the room.

Her calm demeanor and soothing voice relaxed his shoulders, and his breath slowed down. So far, so good.

A noise at the door caught his attention. A tight little body was silhouetted in the entrance—Kelly

Prescott. What the hell? Her yoga pants and loose red T-shirt were sweet, but still sexy. He sat up straighter, and a bead of sweat popped on his brow. Shit, he'd already spoken to the teacher, so he couldn't sneak out.

Maybe she wouldn't notice him. She bent over and selected a cushion—definitely more sexy than sweet in those form-fitting pants. She chose an empty spot on the other side of the circle. Once she'd settled onto her meditation pillow, she looked up and their gazes locked. Her golden eyes slayed him from across the room. Awareness prickled down his spine. Then she winked.

He shifted in his seat, his sweatpants suddenly constricted, as if they'd shrunk three sizes. He pulled his T-shirt down to cover his lap, just in case anybody noticed his dilemma. And had somebody turned up the heat in the room?

Pamela sat down on her own bolster, and the room quieted.

"Welcome, everyone, and thanks for coming to meditation tonight. We've got some newbies, and even we old-timers can do with a refresher before we begin." She gazed around the room and nodded.

"Please close your eyes, rest your hands on your thighs, and shift your attention inside. Start deepening your breath. Tonight we'll practice mantra meditation. The practice is simple, but you'll find it isn't necessarily easy. Do your best and trust in the process."

Christian closed his eyes and worked to regulate and slow down his breathing. Forget the hottest woman he'd ever seen was sitting directly across the circle. In red pants. The red stilettos she'd sported before flashed on the back of his eyelids. What else did she have in red? *Focus, Wolfe. Dammit.*

"Our minds are very active, and we want to give the mind something to do. By repeating a mantra, your mind can begin to quiet. Tonight we'll use the universal mantra 'so hum,' which translates to 'I am.' Inhale on the *so* and exhale on the *hum*. No need to say the word. Simply see it in your mind." Pamela's melodic voice filled the room.

Active was one way to describe the tornado churning through his head. He cracked open one eye and snuck a glance across the circle. Kelly's eyes were closed. As his should be. What? Was he back in junior high? *Focus, dude.*

So hum.

His right ear itched. His hands curled into fists, determined not to fidget or scratch. Could he will the annoying tickle to subside? He managed a few *so hums*.

He could do this. If he could successfully run top-secret missions in Iraq, he could sit still for half an hour, right?

Pins and needles assaulted his left foot with sharp, stabbing pokes. He wiggled his toe, struggling not to move his foot. He was supposed to stay still, damn it. He tried to curl his toes, but then his big toe cramped, and the unrelenting pins and needles persisted with their delicate torture.

Finally, his foot relaxed. *So hum. So hum. So—* A shooting pain attacked his left butt cheek. Despite the cushion, his right glute had gone numb what seemed like hours ago. Was he even on the pillow anymore, or had he somehow crushed it and landed on the solid floor?

So hum. Pamela would probably be calling game

over soon, right?

So hum. Okay, he was getting in the rhythm of this. He could meditate. The tight muscles at the base of his neck softened.

He gagged and resisted the urge to cover his nose with his hand. What was that smell? Rotten eggs? Chili con carne? Had the large guy next to him actually farted?

Oh, who the hell was he kidding? This was a lot harder than he thought it would be.

Probably the most challenging thing he'd ever done. Forget jumping out of planes and officer-training school. He was wired for activity. Vigorous activity. Missions were different because they had a clear goal. Sitting still and breathing for thirty minutes? He'd rather do the mud run at Camp Pendleton.

He didn't even have feet anymore—he couldn't feel either of them. It was okay, as long as the prickling didn't start up again. He risked a deep inhale, and luckily the air smelled normal again. Although he'd choose more carefully who he sat by next time.

What was Kelly doing? He couldn't fight his reaction to her. Once this session was over, he was going to get over his big bad self and ask her out to dinner. Life was too short and why not? Wait. If he was thinking about Kelly, did it mean he wasn't meditating anymore? Shit.

So hum. So hum. So hum.

****

Kelly fidgeted on her meditation cushion. The mantra slipped through her mind like water through a sieve. Unattainable.

"Remember thoughts will arise. The object of

65

meditation isn't to have a blank mind with nothing happening. Rather, when thoughts arise, acknowledge them and return to the mantra." Pamela's soothing voice infused the room.

Ha, acknowledge them? Hers would simply be a teenage girl doodling her boy crush's name in her notebook. Christian Wolfe. Mrs. Christian Wolfe. Kelly Wolfe.

She dug her fingernails into her thighs.

Darn it, she'd always been able to meditate at work. She'd often sneak out and go down and sit in her car in the parking garage for just that purpose. It always helped. In fact, it had been one of the factors enabling her to work at Prescott Law Firm as long as she did. Otherwise, she may have run screaming from the building, as if her pants were on fire, countless times.

Her practice had lapsed during the whole transition—when she needed it most, of course.

So why wasn't she able to focus?

Who was she kidding?

Even though Christian was on the far side of the room, she could sense his presence. He'd looked a little sheepish and slightly embarrassed. Adorable. She shouldn't be thinking about how sexy he was during meditation, but she was only human.

So hum. So hum. So hum.

Why was he here? Just because he was here didn't necessarily mean he had any posttraumatic stress. He seemed fine on the surface, but who knows what those quiet depths concealed? Although at the mention of PTS the other night at dinner, he'd jackknifed off the couch, away from her.

From steamy to subzero in ten seconds flat. Did

she want to be involved with someone who might be battling some serious demons? She exhaled deeply and straightened her spine. Damn it. Enough. But she'd been cautious not to get entangled with anyone who had a tendency toward depression. Or substance abuse issues. Was Christian one of them? She couldn't deny her prior therapist's pronouncement she had codependency issues.

Stop it. Just because he was here to meditate certainly didn't mean he had any issues at all. He was a veteran with an interest in meditation, right? Sophie would have told her if Nick had confided anything, but who knew if the guy code would prevent it. But four tours in Iraq as a commander? How could you not have some demons? Well, how would she ever know unless she got to know him better?

Focus. So hum.

"Begin releasing the mantra slowly. Return to your natural breath," Pamela directed them. "Keep your eyes softly closed for now and simply focus on your inhale and exhale. Take three more full breaths and then slowly open your eyes."

Kelly lifted her eyelids, and his tiger eyes stared directly at her again. Warmth traveled up her spine, and she smiled tentatively at him. The corners of his sensual mouth curved up, softening his strong face.

He took his sweet time putting away his cushion and thanking the teacher. Then he meandered over to where she stood by the door.

"Taking advantage of the work programs?" He smiled again.

"Yup, there's no fancy health club membership attached to my offer, so I figured I'd come in here. How was it for you?" His crisp starched linen, fresh-laundry smell reached her nostrils. It made her want to rub her cheek along his chiseled pecs and snuggle in close.

"Just tell me it gets easier. It was tough." He frowned.

"It does. It just takes practice, like everything else. Some days it goes really smoothly, and the next I can't focus to save my life." *Except focusing on you.*

"Make sure you don't sit next to the guy I did. That's all I'll say." He wrinkled his nose and waved his hand in front of it.

They both laughed and exited the room, heading back toward the building entrance. Her posture relaxed, even though a tingling feeling still permeated her body at his closeness. Under the tough exterior, he was funny.

"What are you doing Saturday?" she blurted out the words. So much for waiting for him to make the first move.

"Saturday?" He angled his head down and arched a thick dark brow. "I'm always at the wine bar Saturday nights—it's our busiest time."

"Oh, of course, of course." *Slow down your breathing, girl.* "I actually meant in the morning. I'm going out to Pups-4-Vets to meet with the founder about partnering with us. Their facility is about an hour east of here, near Menifee. Do you want to come with me? Play with a few dogs?" Whew. There. It wasn't technically a date.

More of a reconnaissance mission. Right.

"Huh. Did Nick mention I was considering getting a dog?" Christian's expression revealed nothing.

"No, he didn't. How great." Convenient for her.

Encouraged, she smiled.

"Sure, I'll go. I just need to be back before two. The group sounds great." He nodded and flashed even white teeth.

"They definitely seem like it. I know they have some dogs who've failed out of training for whatever reason and are available for civilians too." *Subtle, Kelly, subtle.*

"Good to know." The impassive mask slid back into place.

"Well, I was thinking of leaving around eight or eight thirty, if it isn't too early?"

"My body is wired for six a.m., no matter how late I go to bed. So either works. I'm happy to drive." The half smile returned, softening his formidable dark visage.

They'd reached the entrance and paused. Her belly tingled in anticipation at being able to hang out with him for a few hours, to see if a connection existed beyond the immediate physical one. Already the intensity of her attraction to him surpassed any of her prior relationships, even her longest one with Robert.

The trip to the dog rescue was the perfect opportunity to see if they had anything in common besides their friends. And wanting to rip each other's clothes off.

"Great. You know where I live." She returned his smile. "I've got to run back and pick up my stuff." She waved and sauntered back to her office and resisted the temptation to look back to see if he watched her go.

"See you Saturday at oh eight hundred hours," he said.

Chapter 9

Kelly fussed with her hair, smoothing back an errant strand into the messy mermaid-style side braid she'd created. In a mere twenty minutes. Old faded jeans, a slouchy T-shirt, and some sneakers, and she was set. The founder of the rescue group had advised her to dress casually so they could walk the grounds, meet some dogs, and discuss a partnership.

But this morning was potentially her first date with Christian, and clothes gave her confidence. Just as her tailored suits and stilettos powered her court appearances, the appropriate weekend outfit helped settle the skipping of her pulse.

The rumble of a car engine shook her out of her reverie. She headed outside. Christian sat behind the wheel of a sparkling gunmetal-gray Jeep Cherokee. With his mirrored aviator sunglasses and tanned muscular arm resting on the windowsill, he looked like an advertisement for *Outdoors* magazine. She paused for a moment to allow her accelerated heartbeat to slow before heading over to the passenger side of the SUV.

She hopped into the car, and his clean masculine scent surrounded her. What was it about the fresh laundry smell that screamed sex to her? Crips linen sheets to dirty up? Ha. She wiped her now-damp palms on her jeans and fastened her seatbelt before looking at him. Luckily, her sunglasses hid the sheer appreciation and lust in her gaze. *Please let them disguise it.*

"Good morning. Thanks again for driving." She angled in the seat toward him and admired his strong profile.

"Not a problem. Where are we going?" His deep voice was neutral.

"I'll plug the address into the GPS, and she'll guide us there." She tapped the rescue's location into the map, and the automated voice began guiding them down the winding hills and out of Laguna Beach.

"Feel free to choose the music." Yes, he was a man of few words.

She'd restrain her natural tendency to fill the silence with words. Cool, calm, and collected. She leaned forward and selected a heavy-metal-rock station. Metallica barked out it was time for the sandman to enter.

"Nice choice." He aimed a sidelong glance at her but still hadn't smiled.

She grinned. Someone who could appreciate her eclectic taste in music. "Thank you. It's my 'get fired up to kick ass in court' music. The courthouse parking attendant used to crack up when I rolled in dressed in a navy suit and pearls, blasting rock and roll."

"Nice. So why did you move up here?" He kept his gaze on the road, his long tanned fingers gripping the steering wheel.

"Oh, it's a long story. I don't want to bore you." Or reveal too much about my soap-opera family.

"We've got time." He glanced at her again and smiled a crooked smile.

Had she noticed he had a dimple in his right cheek? "Okay, *Reader's Digest* version. My father's kind of a

71

shark." Actually, he'd make the shark in *Jaws* look like a tadpole.

He nodded and gestured with one strong hand for her to continue.

She sighed and glanced out the window. Savored the brisk breeze on her face cooling her now warm cheeks. *Here goes nothing.*

"I was expected to work for the family firm and take it over when my father retires. Let's just say the clients and the cases began to wear on me." She rolled her now tense shoulders back and kept her gaze fastened on the passing scenery. "Everything is about making money or destroying and dismantling what others created. I hit my breaking point last month."

"A particular client or case? Or just in general?" His quiet voice encouraged her.

"In general—for years, actually. I realized I just didn't care about those battles. They seem so meaningless, all about money. I'd always hoped to use my law degree for justice, to help people, to create, to rebuild." She braved a glance at him. He hadn't stopped the car and run for the hills yet. She took a deep breath. She didn't want to divulge too much.

"So you were too idealistic for corporate law, right?" He smiled again.

"Well, in a nutshell, yes. And recently the corruption of some of the clients became too much. I couldn't look at myself in the mirror." She'd had "idealistic woman" tossed at her by her father on countless occasions. He'd used it as an insult, though. Christian made it sound like a strength.

"Why'd you work for your dad, then?" He made it sound so simple.

"Expectations. Family reasons. Cowardice. Guilt. Pressure." Had her dad truly disowned her?

Christian remained silent.

"Look, I lost my older brother. He was being groomed to take over the firm. Once he was gone, it had to be me." And there it was: TMI. She bit her lip, swung her gaze out the window again, and clasped her hands together.

His large, warm hand covered hers and squeezed. Resigned to rejection, startled at the contact, she jolted in her seat and shifted to look at him.

"I'm sorry about your brother. What happened?" His hand stayed over hers.

"Drug overdose. Accidental…we think. It's been twelve years now, and I still wonder if I could have done something differently. Something to save him." She was proud of the steadiness in her voice.

He pressed her hands again and then returned his own to the steering wheel.

They drove in silence for a few moments. The pause wasn't uncomfortable, however. She studied his dark hair, no longer military short, and his erect posture. What was he thinking?

"I'm sorry. I've never lost a sibling, but I lost some of my men in Iraq. Tough to recover." His jaw tightened, and his proud profile looked solemn.

"Yeah." The grief was like a rollercoaster. Would the recurring sadness and memories ever go away? So he'd experienced the bone-crushing grief of losing someone who was struck down too soon.

"I don't know if you are ever quite the same again if you've seen someone die." He shook his head.

"I don't think so." Her heart clenched, and she

gazed out the window again. Sometimes Peter's death seemed like yesterday.

They continued to drive with only the pounding drums and heavy guitar riffs filling the air. So much for a flirtatious drive. But perhaps a true connection nonetheless.

"So did you take the job out of guilt?"

She swiveled to look at him again. Damn, he was persistent. And perceptive. And genuinely seemed interested in her motivation.

"Yup. But recently I learned some things about a big client I couldn't ethically support, and I confronted my dad about it. He told me to grow up or get out. So I got out." She shrugged.

"Huh." He grunted. "Have you talked to him since?"

"No. And probably won't. Can we change the subject? Your turn." She injected a note of levity into her tone. Time to turn this conversation around.

"My turn?"

"Tell me why you resigned your commission early and opened up a wine bar?"

****

Christian swallowed. Damn. Talk about direct.

"Let's just say four tours in the Middle East get to you after a while." *And your men dying or losing a limb doesn't help.*

"I bet. Was it worse than you expected?" Her voice was husky.

"I lost some men. Knowing they'd died because of me made it tough to continue." *And gave me panic attacks, survivor's guilt, and headaches that made me want to rip my head off my body.*

"What? Because of you?" She shifted in her seat, totally focused on him now.

"Yeah, my fault." A familiar tic throbbed at his temple.

"That can't be right. How could it be your fault? They all joined the army voluntarily, right?" Her smooth golden brow creased.

He slammed his hand on the steering wheel. "I was their commanding officer. A major. Responsible for them. They died. One lost his arm. Period." He ground his back teeth and struggled not to let the spear of temper overtake him. Every time he discussed it, which was rare, a knife twisted in his gut.

"I'm sorry. I didn't mean to pry." She shrank back into her seat.

"No, I'm sorry. Look, can we change the subject?" No need to open Pandora's box. He struggled to deepen his breathing and remain calm.

"Tell me about the wine bar." She didn't bat an eyelash at his generally asshole-like behavior. Points for her.

Before he could respond, Kelly pointed a slender golden arm toward a sign proclaiming Pups-4-Vets. "Oh look, there's the entrance."

Timing was everything.

Chapter 10

He pulled into a gravel driveway and bumped along the shadowy tree-lined path until it enlarged into a parking lot. Large pens and grassy dog runs sprawled around the property. Several single-story weathered-wood buildings spread out over what appeared to be several acres. The facilities looked to be older, but they were well tended.

A structure with an enormous red, white, and blue sign had to be the main building. He navigated into a parking space adjacent to a double glass front door, and they exited the car.

Before they could reach the entrance, the door opened and a lanky woman with long dark braids and sturdy black boots approached them. "You must be Ms. Prescott, and who's your friend?" The woman pumped Kelly's hand and smiled at him.

"Call me Kelly, please. This is my friend Christian," she answered before he could reply. Did she really see him as a friend?

"I'm Melinda, and this is my foundation. Thanks for coming out. Do you want to take a walk around first and see some of the dogs?" She sauntered toward one of the other buildings, and they fell into place behind her. "We've got a few training sessions happening, so you can see how it all works here," she called over her shoulder.

Kelly shrugged. The dogs, it was.

The awkwardness from the car had dissipated, but the confidences she'd shared about her brother troubled him. How much guilt did she carry if she had taken the job with her family's firm to make up for the death of her brother? He respected her sense of duty but feared her heavy burden remained. His own guilt definitely did.

Melinda stopped at a pen where a husky young man worked with some type of creature. Was it a rat? Or some exotic pig? Certainly not a service dog with those bulging eyes and lolling tongue.

"Hey, Howard, how's it going with Olive?" Melinda called to the trainer.

Olive? Seriously? The tiny beast had eyes like two oversized black olives. How could a fur ball be of service?

"Hey." Howard offered a half wave and ambled over. "Come on in, and I'll show you."

"Hi, sweetie." Kelly cooed at the little piglet and reached down to scratch behind its mismatched ears.

It ignored her and swiveled its grizzled head, latching those crazy bug eyes onto him. With a series of small yips, it charged at him, leapt onto its back legs, and pawed at his shin.

What the hell? He didn't have to pet the thing, did he?

"She likes you." Kelly laughed as she pushed to her feet. "She wants nothing to do with me."

"You can pet her or pick her up," Howard said. "She won't bite you."

"Bite me?" No way in hell was he touching that thing.

"You aren't scared of dogs, are you?" Melinda asked with a frown and a sideways glance at Kelly.

"Scared? Of this? No." Still, he didn't bend down to pet the alien-looking object. He didn't want to encourage her attentions.

Kelly leaned in to pet Olive, and her hand brushed his denim-clad leg. Even through the heavy material, a spark of heat ignited and shot straight up his thigh. Damn. Maybe the dog was safer?

Olive shifted her attention to his other leg and began dancing a little jig. What the hell was wrong with it?

"Come on, Christian. Just pick her up. Poor thing seems to be half in love with you." Kelly laughed again.

"Oh fine." He leaned down and grasped the little beast by its plump midsection. "What is it? Not really a dog, right?"

He held the ten pounds of fur aloft, and it locked its bug eyes onto his. Was she grinning at him? Her pink tongue lolled out of the right side of her mouth.

"Give her a little hug. Don't just hold her out there." Melinda's brisk tone brooked no argument.

Geez. Fine. He snuggled the dog against his shoulder, and he could have sworn she sighed in ecstasy. She laid her head on his shoulder and gazed up at him. Even he could see the worship in her eyes. Figures this ugly little creature would latch onto him. He gave a few gentle pats to the rolls of fat on her back and set her down.

"There. Are you happy?" He glanced at Kelly, who was grinning, looking incredibly gorgeous. He'd much rather snuggle her sexy little body into his shoulder.

"Are you sure it's a dog? And how could it help a

disabled vet?" He directed his gaze at Melinda. Weren't service dogs usually Labs or other large breeds who could provide physical assistance if needed?

"I'll tell you. Come on. We'll let Olive and Howard finish training while we continue the tour." Melinda headed back toward the metal gate, and they trailed behind her.

Before they could exit the pen, Olive darted out and slammed against his ankles. He peered down, and sure enough she was gazing up at him with stars in her Bette Davis eyes. She hopped and yipped, apparently wanting to be carried. Some service dog.

"Olive, go back to Howard," Melinda commanded.

"We're about done, so she can follow along with you on the tour," Howard called with a smirk on his freckled face.

"Great," he muttered. Olive looked up at him in triumph and marched next to him. He'd probably trip over her and break his neck.

"Different breeds are good for different types of issues," Melinda explained as they toured the grounds. "For example, larger dogs like Labrador retrievers and Bernese mountain dogs are good for people confined to a wheelchair or maybe those with prosthetic limbs. But as you know, a lot of the conditions these soldiers return to our country with aren't necessarily visible injuries. The statistics on soldiers committing suicide and falling into drug and alcohol addiction are staggering."

"Exactly. It's why I'm so passionate about this program and so interested in partnering with you, Melinda. I've always been big into animal rescue. I was the kid who constantly came home with the wounded bird." Kelly nodded, her full pink mouth drawn into a straight line.

"Well, I'm so glad you are because we've been trying to partner with Peaceful Warrior for a long time, and they just didn't have the manpower to get out here like you have. And so quickly too." Melinda smiled, her lean cheeks creasing.

"I'm really excited. We don't have time to lose. So keep explaining about the smaller dogs. I can't imagine sweet little Olive with someone in a wheelchair, unless she was riding in it." Kelly beamed down at the dog plastered to his side.

What was with this damned little pig-rat?

"I think you've got an admirer, Christian. She's never taken to someone like this before." Melinda laughed as she looked down at Olive. "Anyway, Olive is a pug, and pugs are really great for people with anxiety and depression. They're very loyal, loving, and they have an excellent sixth sense for anxiety. It's like they tune into blood pressure and adrenaline and all the senses."

"Well, animals are intuitive that way, but seriously, what can she do for it?" Christian interjected. Melinda was certainly correct about how many of the scars weren't visible to the naked eye. Like his.

"Of course, there aren't the same kinds of tangibles as, say, the Lab who learns to open doors, help someone in a wheelchair and such, but they offer comfort. They can sense if you are stressed out and come sit in your lap or cuddle. Studies reflect how the simple act of petting an animal lowers your blood pressure and relieves anxiety. And in terms of helping with depression—a dog loves you unconditionally, so you no longer feel completely alone in the world."

"Huh." Was Olive bonded to him because she sensed he had issues?

They finished the tour and headed back into the office. Not surprisingly, Olive escorted them. They sat down around a well-used conference room table, and Kelly and Melinda discussed the parameters of the partnership between Peaceful Warrior and Pups-4-Vets.

Olive squeaked and rose onto her hind legs, tilting her head coquettishly. If she'd had long hair, she probably would have flipped it over her shoulder.

Fine. He'd pick her up. Just for a little bit.

He placed her on his lap, and she circled twice and settled down. She gazed up at him in adoration, licked his hand, and promptly laid her head down and began snoring. Loudly. He stroked her wiry fur, expecting it to feel like steel wool, and was surprised at how silky it actually was.

"Found a new friend?" Kelly asked. She and Melinda had watched the whole exchange. Damn it.

"Well, she was pestering me. I figured she could sit here while you guys get this finished." It sounded lame, even to his own ears.

"Sure..." Kelly drawled out the word before she turned back to Melinda.

"Don't get too attached, Christian," Melinda said. "We've invested a lot into her training, and she'll need to be adopted by a veteran. We've got a few other cute dogs, though, who've failed out of training you might want to meet. It looks like you're in the market?"

"Well, Christian is a veteran—" Kelly bit her lip.

"Really? Why didn't you mention it?" Melinda's eyes widened. Now they were both staring at him again.

Great.

"Yeah, retired major."

"Why didn't you say so? But she needs to be adopted by someone who needs her. She's been trained…" Melinda's brow lowered as she attempted to let him down easy.

"I need her," he blurted out. Damn it. Something about this little beast tugged at him. Hadn't she picked him?

"Can you share why?" Melinda looked between him and Kelly.

"Do you want me to leave the room for a few minutes while you talk?" Kelly's eyes deepened to dark honey pools.

Damn it. "No, no, it's fine." He sighed. "I was diagnosed with posttraumatic stress when I resigned my commission. Maybe it's why she's drawn to me. She can tell." Olive burrowed deeper against his belly.

"Can you give me more details? We usually have a battery of tests we run."

"I've got the paperwork and can share it. Mostly nightmares and anxiety." Like Stephen King-type scenarios, no big deal. Right.

"Depression? Suicidal thoughts?" Melinda's voice was matter of fact.

He remained laser focused on her, avoiding looking at Kelly, although her gaze burned into him. Maybe sharing the truth would be enough to send her running in the opposite direction, which was probably the smartest avenue for her. "No. The dreams and the panic attacks strike me at weird times of the day." The muscles between his shoulder blades tightened, and beads of sweat formed on the back of his neck. Better she knew now.

"How do you handle them now?"

"During the day? Intense workouts or getting to the beach. At night? Get up and stay awake until I can try to sleep again. I just started meditating." He slowed down his exhales, recalling the meditation teacher's advice.

Olive grunted and shifted in his lap. He looked down at her, and she cracked open one love-filled eye. He hadn't seen that look on a female's face since his family dog, Marnie, when he was a boy. The enormous mutt had adored him, and the feeling had been mutual. She'd followed him everywhere. Slept with him. When he'd left for college, he'd shed rare tears into Marnie's velvety fur. Oh hell, Olive was coming home with him today.

"Okay, it does sound like Olive could be a good fit for you. But we have protocols and procedures. I can give you the paperwork, you send it back to me, and we'll go from there."

"No. She's coming with me today. I'll fill out the paperwork now. I'll send you over my medical records." He squeezed Olive against him. Damn it, he wasn't leaving without her.

"I can vouch for him, Melinda. I think Olive might be inconsolable if we separated them today," Kelly said, her smile wide.

"Well, this is highly unusual, but I know dogs better than I know most people, and you're right. She's wildly infatuated with you. Let me go get the paperwork for you to start on." Melinda shrugged her narrow shoulders and scooted her chair away from the table.

"And if we've got a deal, I've got the Peaceful Warrior partnership agreement as well." Kelly reached for her briefcase.

"Great. I'll be right back." Melinda headed out of the conference room.

"So you've fallen in love at first sight. Who would've figured?" Kelly joked.

"It's not love. Don't be ridiculous." Olive opened both eyes and pouted. "Okay, fine, there's something about her."

"I think it's great. I've always wanted a dog but never had the time with work." She focused on the documents she retrieved from her briefcase, not meeting his eyes.

"I haven't had one since I was a kid. Marnie. She died when I was in college. Never made sense to get another one before now, but I can take her to Vines with me." She wouldn't be a health violation, would she?

"Awww, you should get one of those little pink backpacks and carry her around with you." Kelly giggled.

"Funny. It would have to be camouflage." He laughed. After this day, who knew? The tension between his shoulders dissipated, and his pulse was slow and steady.

Melinda returned with a thick sheaf of papers and plunked them and a pen down in front of him.

"Get to work on those while Kelly and I get the partnership agreement hammered out."

Damn, there were more pages to the adoption application and agreement than to his release papers from the military. He got to work. Olive didn't budge.

After about an hour, they completed their respective paperwork. Melinda and Kelly shook hands, agreement complete. Then Melinda gave him a hot-pink flowered leash to take Olive home with—as if the dog wouldn't ride shotgun on his lap on the way home.

They climbed back into his jeep, and Kelly flashed her brilliant white smile. "Want me to play nanny and hold your baby while you drive?"

"Very funny." He chuckled. Somehow, her smartass sense of humor made her even more beautiful. He fired up the car, and together they headed back to Laguna.

Chapter 11

"Do you want to stop at the pet store on the way back? I can help you make sure Olive gets everything she needs, like a pink studded collar, some frilly dresses to accompany you to the wine bar, and a backpack." Kelly's shoulders shook, and she couldn't prevent a snort of laughter picturing Christian dressing Olive in a frilly puppy tutu.

"A dress? There is no way in hell my dog will ever wear a dress." His jaw dropped, and he flicked his gaze at her.

"A tiara, then?" She laughed. Had she actually shocked him?

"Should I just take you home now?" His lips quirked up at the corners.

"No, no. Don't worry. I won't force you to outfit her in ruffles. But can I use you two as my first testimonial for the collaboration with Pups-4-Vets? It's a great story."

"No." He barked the word. "No, I'd rather you don't share about my deal. Nobody knows, and I want to keep it my business." His tone was soft, but resolute.

"Nobody?" Her smile faded, and her enthusiasm slipped a notch.

"Well, yeah, but only my family and a few close friends." His knuckles turned white where his long tanned fingers gripped the steering wheel. "The wine bar is my business now, and there's no need to reveal my crap."

"It's not crap—"

"You don't have any idea what it is, so, no." His tone chilled.

Olive scrambled off her lap and waddled over the console. With a high-pitched yip, she sprawled out onto Christian's lap. He reached down one hand and stroked the dog's head.

"I'm sorry. Of course if you don't want me to tell anyone, I won't. But I hate that you see this as a flaw. Do you want to tell me any more about it? I'm a really good listener." Didn't he see how strong he was? Had anyone comforted him?

"We're almost to the pet store. Do you mind making a list?" He shook his head and changed the subject.

Case closed.

****

Christian steered the car up one of the charming winding little streets that seemed to dominate Laguna Beach. He pulled into a paved driveway and parked in front of a beautiful gleaming wooden garage door. A well-manicured lawn framed a slate-gray, single-story craftsman-style bungalow with an enormous cherry-red front door. She loved it instantly.

"Hi, lucky little girl, we're home." The dog had deigned to perch in Kelly's lap on the drive back from the pet store. The second the car stopped, Olive leapt off her lap into his arms.

He laughed and gazed down at the silly-looking creature. He didn't realize it yet, but the love affair between him and Olive was mutual. Warmth curled in her center—he was so handsome with his five-o'clock shadow and carved-from-marble jawline.

The contrast between his Special Forces macho exterior and his soft toasted-marshmallow center, at least where the dog was concerned, melted her heart. Just when she thought he couldn't appear more attractive—

"Let me pop the back door and grab all her stuff." He laughed as he looked into the back seat of the SUV.

Heat rose to her cheeks. Had he caught her ogling him? Again? The dog. Help with the pet supplies. No sexy business going on around here, nope. She hopped out of the car and smoothed her hair back. Keep it light. He wasn't exactly lusting after her.

He carried Olive like a Nerf football under one sinewy-bronzed arm.

"I've got a few bags… I'm right behind you." She followed him along the natural paver-stoned walkway to the cheerful front door. Bougainvillea crept up the stone chimney and along sparkling windows in the front of the house. Every inch of the house was pristine. Her obsessive-compulsive little soul danced with joy.

He managed to keep Olive snuggled under his arm, dropped the bags, and opened the door. They entered a small foyer that immediately expanded into a large great room dominated by a cream shaker stone fireplace with a driftwood mantle, an enormous L-shaped couch, and a bright George Rodrigue painting of Blue Dog highlighted by creamy white walls. Built-ins were stuffed full of books of all shapes and sizes, and piles of paperbacks littered the coffee and end tables.

"I love your Blue Dog. I've always wanted one of his paintings. And you weren't kidding when you said you liked to read." His home was cozy yet disciplined: order existed everywhere except for the explosion of books. Another thing they shared.

"Right? Have a seat and I'll grab the bags." He handed her the dog, who squirmed to be let down.

"Hold on, little girl. Your papa will be right back." She cooed at the pup who wiggled out of her arms and scampered to the front door, completely ignoring her.

Christian returned with more bags and the circular red fleece dog bed, kicking the front door shut behind him. She'd tried to convince him to buy the pink-flowered one, but he'd objected on principle.

He plopped the bed down by the couch and headed toward the kitchen, which opened from the living room. She admired the gray-taupe hardwood floors as she trailed behind him, studiously attempting not to stare at his perfect butt.

"Let me put some of this away and get her set up. I'm starved. Do you have time for pizza and wine?" He began pulling items out of the bags. Shiny ceramic food and water bowls, stuffed toys, miniature bones, and an enormous sack of food that would last for a year. Olive was the official lottery winner.

"I'd love to, but do you have time before work?" She almost drooled over his immaculate kitchen. Could it actually be as organized as her own? Why was it sexy?

"I've got some time." He still had his head buried in one of the bags.

"Veggie okay?" It had to be a good sign he wanted to hang out longer, didn't it?

"My favorite. Can you order a salad too?" His words were muffled.

"A salad? Sure, where's a good place to order from?"

"Oh, I forgot you're new to Laguna. Call Paoli's. They've got the best delivery." He whipped his head out of the bag and flashed straight white teeth.

The small lines around his shimmering tiger eyes fanned out when he smiled, and the warm gold dominated the green now. Her stomach flip-flopped, and she turned away and dug her phone out of her briefcase before she did drool.

After she ordered, she pivoted back toward the counter, where he was snuggling Olive against his shoulder. The dog grinned against his tanned neck. Lucky girl.

"They said twenty minutes."

"Great, let's pick some wine. Cab or a red blend?"

She followed him into a room showcasing wine in floor-to-ceiling glass-fronted shelves. "Um, how do you pick? What is that, three hundred bottles?" Precisely organized tags classified each vintage.

"Closer to three hundred and fifty…" His grin was sheepish. "What can I say? I love wine."

"Me too, but wow. Are these all personal, or do any go to Vines?" Could he really be cellaring all this wine?

"All mine." He cradled a bottle in his free arm. "Far Niente, a special bottle for a special day."

"Fancy wine for a fancy puppy. I'm sure Olive will approve." She laughed. He certainly had top-of-the-line taste in just about everything.

"Well, it's your fault for inviting me out there. You have to celebrate with me." He set Olive down and strolled toward the kitchen island.

He uncorked the wine and poured it into two stemless red wineglasses. He offered one to her, his long fingers brushing hers. A chill danced up her arm and skipped down her spine.

"Are you cold?" He raised a dark brow.

"No, no, I'm fine." *Not attracted to you at all, nope, not one little bit.*

"Here's to new beginnings." They clinked glasses.

"New beginnings. So do you miss it?" She needed to shift her attention away from her body's over-the-top reactions.

"Miss it?" One dark eyebrow winged up.

"Being a leader in the military, going on missions, the adrenaline rush?" *Great, conjure up the Middle East. Way to kill the attraction.* Why couldn't she shut up?

"It's an adjustment." He paused and sipped his wine.

Crickets.

The doorbell rang, interrupting the awkward silence. Olive raced to answer it with him.

"Get ready for the best pizza of your life." He returned and set the box down and flipped open the lid. Fragrant steam wafted up from the enormous pie.

"Mmmmmm…it smells delicious." Her mouth watered in anticipation. Pizza was safer than staring at Christian Wolfe any day, right?

"Tastes as good as it smells." He grabbed a slice and bit half of it in one mouthful, then held it out to her. "C'mon. Try it."

She inhaled sharply. *Dangerous territory ahead.* She sank her teeth into it, but a long string of melted cheese dribbled down her chin and squashed the potential sensuality of the moment. Her hand flew up to catch the hot mess now decorating the lower half of her face. He stroked his thumb along her jawline at the same time, singeing her with his touch.

"Oh no—" She jerked back and grasped for a napkin to wipe away the sauce. Her heartbeat galloped in her chest, and she simply stared into his eyes, which had darkened.

"My fault." He slowly lowered his hand and shifted away from her. "You can't get good pizza in the Middle East. Trust me, the second we hit US soil, we all headed out for pizza first thing."

Talk about a segue. But he'd volunteered information about his time overseas for the first time. She accepted the rest of the slice of pizza, careful to avoid his searing touch. They ate in silence for a few minutes. She looked up, and he was staring at her.

As if he'd like to take his next bite out of her, not the pizza.

He set down his slice and leaned forward. Cupping her face in one hand, he gently brushed his lips against hers and pressed a few featherlight kisses on each corner of her mouth. Warmth rose on her cheeks, and lightning sparked through her veins.

At her response, he deepened the kiss, opening her lips and stroking her tongue with his. Thoughts shut down and sensation took over. With a murmur low in her throat, she slid off her stool and landed right between his strong thighs. She wound her arms around his neck, never breaking contact with his yummy mouth. He tasted like wine and pizza, an irresistible combination. He threaded his other hand through her hair, holding her head in place.

His fresh scent enveloped her, and all that remained were his firm sensual lips learning every inch of her mouth. Her skin tingled where his hand caressed her jaw. When his hands stroked down her back, flames burned through her thin T-shirt. He tugged her hips into his unmistakable arousal, and her center liquefied.

He withdrew with a husky laugh and rested his forehead against hers for a sweet moment. Their combined panting punctuated the air. Kelly retreated to her stool, welcoming the support beneath her shaky legs. Maybe her head would stay attached to her body, but she wasn't sure.

Olive yipped, and he picked the dog up and settled her on his lap. He reached out a hand and covered hers in a firm grip. "I'd like to see you again, Kelly. Want to take the beast on a hike tomorrow? Maybe grab breakfast first?"

"Breakfast?" *Breakfast*, as in was he inviting her to stay over and wanted her to know it wouldn't be a one-night stand, or just breakfast as part of a date? Damn her overanalytical brain.

"Like a date tomorrow. I've got to get to the wine bar soon. But I'd like to see you again." His sincere gaze pinned her to the spot.

"I've got a little work to do, but I'd love to hike. Do you think Olive will be okay here while you go to Vines, or are you bringing her with you?" She'd totally forgotten he had to work tonight. She'd been so enthralled with his words, wine, and kisses, she'd lost track of time.

"I'll set her up here. Once she's a little more settled, I'm sure I'll bring her in." He smiled again, and her heartbeat accelerated again. When his stern demeanor softened, he was dangerously handsome.

"Okay, well, I'll let you get ready for work." She rose and headed over to get her briefcase.

He strode across the room in two long strides, his rangy body covering the large room before she could open the door. He grasped her shoulders and captured another mind-blowing kiss.

"I picked you up, remember? Let me run you back to the cottage." He grinned.

"Oh yeah." She struggled to think clearly. "Great, thanks."

When he pulled up at her home, he flashed his sexy grin again. "Tomorrow around nine okay?"

"Sure. Well, have a good night." Where was her usual confident repartee? Lost after the pizza encounter? She half waved and prayed she didn't trip and fall flat on her face on the way to her door.

"Sweet dreams," Christian called from the car.

He'd definitely be in her dreams, but she wasn't certain they'd be sweet.

Chapter 12

Christian pulled up to Kelly's cottage at two minutes before nine. When the rumble of the engine shut off, Olive peered up at him from his lap. Who knew this little ten-pound beast would already have him wrapped around her tiny paw? While he was deciding whether to move her to the passenger seat or simply carry her to Kelly's cottage, the front door opened.

When Kelly stepped out onto the porch, his heart thundered in his chest. She grabbed him by the throat, and not just because of the way her tawny skin and curvy petite figure filled out a pair of stretchy red capri workout pants and a fitted white tank. She strolled up to the driver's side and leaned in and scratched Olive's ears and crooned to the delighted dog. Her slender hand was dangerously close to his lap. Olive's curly tail wagged madly and luckily camouflaged just how happy he was to see Kelly, too.

She flashed him a smile. "Hi, sorry I'm late, but I got caught up doing a little work and lost track of time." She hurried over to the passenger side and slid into the front seat.

"You made it with one minute to spare." He managed a tight smile and attempted to adjust the dog over his now-uncomfortable lap.

To disguise his over-the-top reaction, he reversed and shot out of the driveway in a quick maneuver that left her gasping. Would that be how she sounded when they were in bed?

"Go, Speed Racer, go." She joked but double-checked her seat belt to ensure it was fastened.

Her sweet cinnamon scent wafted toward him. Damn, he could swallow her up in one gulp.

"How was the first night with little Olive?" Kelly grinned when one of the dog's crooked ears perked up.

"Honestly? I slept better last night than I have in ages." Since before Iraq.

"And did she sleep with you or in her own bed?" She laughed, as if she already knew the answer.

"Busted. She needed some reassurance after I left her last night, so I let her come onto the bed for a while." Having her plump, warm body snuggled against him had felt amazing. Right now, the dog's current unwillingness to move was the only thing saving him from completely embarrassing himself.

"And one thing led to another... I get it." Her teasing tone caused a tightening in his chest.

The glowing sun smiled on them from the cloudless azure sky as they cruised in companionable silence down Pacific Coast Highway. The salty ocean breeze flowed through the open windows and lifted strands of Kelly's silky hair. He appreciated her ability to simply be instead of filling space with meaningless chatter. But she intrigued him. "So work on a Sunday morning?" Was that the best he could do? *Apparently.*

"Frankly, the files are a disaster. It's going to take me some extra time to get organized. And I'm implementing the new partnership with Pups-4-Vets, and I've got ideas for several more services. I've also got some pending lawsuits, contracts that should've been signed months ago… It's going to take a while to get everything organized. Peaceful Warrior used an outside law firm before, and now I'm trying to consolidate it all." She shifted in her seat to look at him and smoothed an errant strand of hair behind her ear. "I'm sorry. This must be really boring." A small line formed between her eyebrows.

"Not boring at all. Go on." Her husky voice could recite the California Tax Code, and he'd be turned on.

"I told you I'm a major dork. I'm creating an organizational structure just for myself. Without anyone standing over my shoulder and breathing down my neck. I feel free for the first time in my career." Joy threaded through her voice.

"I get it. I like owning my own business. I'm still in charge, but it's not the military." And he realized he did. He certainly wasn't saving lives or running covert missions as he had in Iraq, but he was providing enjoyment and a place for people to spend a few hours of leisure time. Nobody to answer to except for himself.

"Right? Mr. Williams wants me to run the show. Well, I do have to set up a meeting with the board of directors and present my proposals and projections and such, but it's okay. I can be accountable once a quarter." She laughed.

"Have you ever thought of running your own firm?" With her confidence and obvious pleasure in her work, she could conquer the world.

"Nope, at least not yet. I've just gotten out from under my father's thumb, and now I'm learning as much as I can about the vets, what we can do, how to be part of a nonprofit. Lots to do." Her eyes clouded when she brought up her father.

"The more organizations designed to help out with the transition, the better." He paused, unaccustomed to sharing his military experiences, but with her, somehow the words flowed more freely. "You'll see once you're at Peaceful Warrior a while. A lot of soldiers can't assimilate back into civilian life."

She reached over and stroked his forearm. He jolted at the frisson of energy from her touch and snapped his head to look at her.

"I'm glad you made it back in one piece." Her full lips curved up, and she brushed his arm one more time before withdrawing her delicate hand and placing it on her lap.

"Me too." The back of his neck heated, and he glued his gaze to the road, determined not to allow his imagination to run wild. If only she were on his lap and Olive over in the passenger seat.

Well, he'd slam into a tree or the guardrail if that were the case.

He headed east on the 133, and as they left the ocean in the rearview mirror, the terrain grew hillier. He slowed when the entrance to the hiking area appeared and cruised into a parking lot shrouded in trees and sprinkled with a few picnic tables.

"This is Laguna Coast Wilderness Park. It's got some great hiking trails, so we'll see what Olive's made of."

"It's gorgeous, and I'm surprised how close it is to town. I predict you may be carrying her the whole way." Kelly laughed again.

They parked, and he popped the SUV's back door and pulled out sunscreen and a few bottles of water. They slathered on lotion, and he couldn't rip his gaze from her delicate long, slender fingers. His entire body stiffened again, visualizing those fingers wrapped around him.

"Christian?" She stared at him, her eyebrows arched over her dark sunglasses.

"Huh?" He snapped back to the present moment. Busted.

"Do my shoulders, please? I always seem to miss around my tank-top straps." She handed him the bottle and angled her toned back toward him while bundling her hair into a high ponytail.

His teeth clicked together, and surprise registered when he didn't break every single one. Had he lost every iota of self-control? His years in the military seemed like another lifetime. He rolled back his shoulders and dug deep. He could do this.

Her satiny skin was warm under his fingers, and he massaged the cool lotion on to her taut muscles.

"Mmmm." She leaned her head to one side. The downy hairs dusting her golden nape beckoned to him.

He caught himself seconds before he nibbled on her like a cinnamon pastry. He yanked his hands away and stumbled backwards. "You ready?" he asked. They needed to hike. He needed something else to focus on so he didn't pounce on her.

They set off down the trail with Olive alternating threading between his ankles and trotting up ahead, making sure she stopped to sniff each bush, tree, and rock. Christian was hyperaware of Kelly's proximity as they hiked the narrow path. Left, right, left, right. One foot in front of the other. *Don't grab her and kiss her.* Where was this focus when he'd tried to meditate?

Suddenly, Kelly stumbled and nose-dived toward

the ground. He grabbed her with both hands and hauled her back, just saving her before she sprawled flat on her face. Her firm curves fit against him perfectly, from the delectable shoulders down to her tiny waist and her rounded bottom. His arms circled her, and he couldn't stop himself from nuzzling her tempting neck.

"Christian..." Her fingers curled around his arms. And her fingernails dug in. He pulled her closer, grazed his mouth over the tender skin along her delicate collarbone. "Oh my God, that feels amazing. Don't stop."

He whipped her around and yanked her hips into his, groaning at how perfectly she fit against him. With one hand holding her firmly against him, he grasped her silky ponytail and tugged her head back and plundered her mouth. She rubbed against him, plunged her fingers into his hair, and dragged him closer. His mind went blank as hot sensation took over.

****

She was lost. Lost in the circle of his powerful arms banded around her. Lost in the heat of his passionate kiss. Lost in the scent of his clean masculine skin mingled with sunscreen and sweat. His hair was lush and thick between her fingers, and his rigid arousal dug into her belly. He paused and brought both hands up to frame her face, his eyes heavy lidded and now molten green as he stared into hers. With a growl, he captured her mouth again, and his minty breath mingled with hers.

Tingles traveled from the soles of her feet and spiraled up her spine. She clung to his broad shoulders, his powerful physique her anchor. From a distance, a faint sound infiltrated her consciousness. Yapping. Still, she couldn't make herself pull away from his delicious mouth.

The tingles changed to tremors, and her feet were no longer rooted to the rock-strewn path. She wasn't trembling in his arms. The earth was shifting beneath their feet. High-pitched barks penetrated her brain, and sharp claws scratched at her bare calves. Olive. What the hell was happening?

The rumbling increased, trees rattled, and pebbles bubbled along the path. Christian gripped her shoulders and looked around wildly as the din escalated to a thunderous crescendo. The dog's howling grew, and she vaulted up against Christian's legs.

Suddenly, a deafening crack, louder than the Metallica concert she'd seen a few years ago, blasted Kelly's eardrums. Christian yanked her to the ground with him, covering her with his body and clutching his hands against his ears. Olive flattened herself into the space between them. A tree branch thudded to the ground, and leaves shrouded them. Kelly clung to him as the earth continued to rock and roll beneath them.

Everything grew still, and in the eerie silence, his heavy weight continued to pin her down. Olive licked his face, but he remained immobile.

"Christian?" Kelly stroked his back. "It's okay. It's okay." No reply. A chill shot down her spine when he failed to respond.

Olive renewed her exertions—lick, bark, lick, bark. Finally, their combined efforts must have penetrated. He shifted to a seated position and dropped his head into his hands, shaking it back and forth. When he looked up at her, his eyes no longer glowed with passion; instead, they were glazed, unseeing.

"Christian, are you okay?" Her heart clenched. His expression remained blank and unfocused. "It was a small earthquake. We're fine. We're fine." She continued to soothe him, stroking her hand along his shoulder. *Please let him be okay.*

He sucked in a few ragged breaths and raked his sweat-dampened hair away from his pale face.

"Give me a minute." His deep voice was hoarse and barely a whisper.

She looked around. Tree branches and leaves were scattered around them, but nothing moved. Living in San Diego, she'd learned there could be aftershocks and feared another quake lay in wait for them. Time to get Christian out of the woods. Immediately.

"We're fine. Everything is fine. I think it sounded a lot worse than it actually was." She snapped to her feet and pasted on a cheerful smile in case he actually looked at her again.

He finally looked up, and Olive took the opportunity to hop into his lap. She burrowed against him, and he stroked her wiry fur. His enormous pupils began to shrink, but he didn't utter a syllable. He rose to his feet with Olive tucked under one arm.

"Do you mind if we skip the rest of the hike? The quake was a little intense." Kelly hugged her arms around her waist.

"Are you sure?" His skin remained pale, and he looked ten years older than he had an hour ago, the laugh crinkles around his eyes suddenly deep creases.

"Definitely. I'll never get used to having even the occasional earthquake. I've never been around for a big one, but you just never know." She slanted her gaze toward him and summoned her impassive lawyer face.

No need for him to see her freaking out inside.

"Yeah, let's head back." He pivoted and marched toward the parking lot.

He wasn't the passionate man who had blown her socks off a short while earlier. Determination fueled her pace. Purpose flooded her brain. She would help him. Pamper him.

"I'm happy to drive if you want," Kelly offered once they reached his SUV. Christian appeared vulnerable.

"Yeah. I've got a bitch of a headache." His face remained grim. His T-shirt was drenched with sweat, and strands of dark hair clung to his forehead.

"I know earthquakes can be really stressful, but I'll make sure everything's okay. Do you need help getting in the car?"

"No." He barked the reply and strode to the passenger door. "Let's just go, okay?" Irritation threaded through his tone.

She jumped and swallowed back an apology. *Crap, way to go, Kelly.* They got into the car, and she fumbled to adjust the seat so she could actually reach the pedals. Christian leaned his head back on the seat and remained silent while Olive settled into his lap. Thank goodness the dog was offering comfort.

"I'm sorry to bug you, but what's the fastest way home?" She studied his profile, his clenched jaw, his shoulders slumped against the seat.

"Use the GPS." Coldness iced his tone.

"Sure, sure. Sorry." She bit her lip and punched the address into her phone's GPS. Why couldn't she say the right thing? Comfort him somehow?

Unable to bear the heavy silence, after a few

minutes she turned on the radio.

"No radio." His eyes remained shut, and his voice monosyllabic.

"I'm sorry. Can I do anything?" Her hands trembled on the steering wheel, and her stomach performed an uneasy roll.

"Just stop talking. Please." Each syllable landed like a slap.

The remainder of the drive back to her cottage stretched interminably. His breath was unsteady, and his head remained turned away from her. Damn.

A memory of picking up her brother Peter after an egregious bender slammed into her. One of his friends, who'd actually been semisober, had called her and said she should come and pick up her brother. As usual, she ran to the rescue. He'd mixed several different drugs, and when she arrived, he was twitching on a couch, deathly pale, and practically foaming at the mouth. With the help of his so-called friend, she'd managed to wrestle him into her car and sped to the emergency room. He'd gripped her arm and begged her not to, pleaded for her to take him home. So she'd nursed him and watched over him until she felt safe leaving him the following morning.

She shook herself back to the present. Christian wasn't her brother, nor was he a drug addict. She wasn't his caretaker. She was his...his what? Friend? Definitely not his girlfriend.

She parked in front of her cottage. He didn't budge when she flicked off the ignition.

"Christian, do you want to come in for a while? Lie down? Or I could get you an ice pack, some aspirin?"

"I'm not a child. I'm fine," he snapped, opening his

eyes. The beautiful green gold had chilled to chips of glacial ice.

She shivered. "I'm sorry." She began releasing her seatbelt. Time to retreat.

"And damn it, stop apologizing."

"I'm—" She bit her lip before she could say sorry again. Her stomach churned, and her fingers fumbled on the seatbelt latch.

He thumped his head against the seat and then turned to look at her. "I'm sorry. I just need to be by myself. And I don't think seeing each other again is a good idea." His expression revealed nothing.

"What?" She couldn't prevent the catch in her voice.

"I don't want to see you again." He unbuckled his seatbelt and got out of the car.

She climbed out slowly and backed away from the car. A buzzing filled her ears, and her limbs began to quake again. Without another glance or word, he climbed in and drove away.

She wrapped her arms around herself, her stomach a roiling pit, and watched his car's taillights disappear.

Chapter 13

Christian shook his head, cursing as the rivulets of sweat pouring down his forehead obscured his vision. He had only completed fifty pull-ups, and he couldn't stop until he'd reached one hundred. Wouldn't stop. Fine, he'd do them blind. What did he need to see anyway?

He squeezed his eyes shut and continued to lower his body and wrench it back up. Behind the black lens of his eyelids, the recurrent nightmare flashed again.

He crouched behind the corner of the crumbling building, breathing as quietly as possible. The way he'd been trained. Feel invisible, act invisible, remain undiscoverable. But the beating of his heart pounded in his temples like relentless thunder, and he prayed nobody else could hear the staccato tempo. He sprinted across the courtyard littered with debris, careful to avoid any of the blasted concrete slabs littering the ground. Out of his peripheral vision, he could discern his top two guys in position. They moved as one toward the entryway of the semidemolished structure. They made a run for the door, staying pressed close against the walls, and scooted closer toward what he hoped was the inner sanctum. Minimal time for this critical mission. No room to fail.

Suddenly, the iron door imploded. Flames and bits of rubble flew everywhere. He ducked, shielding his head with his arms, but burning shards of metal sliced into him even through his bulletproof clothing. The interminable blast pierced his eardrums, and he burned from the heat and the pungent odor of smoke and sulfur.

Just as quickly, silence reigned. He opened and closed his fingers. They were all still attached so that was a good thing. He looked around, his head moving in slow motion as if he were dragging it through molasses. Moisture blinded him, and he swiped at his forehead under his hard helmet. He looked at his hand. Blood dripped from his fingers.

He rubbed furiously but couldn't stop the deluge. He struggled to his feet, dread filling him at the eerie quiet. Where were his guys? Dark smoke billowed out from the blasted doorway, but nobody emerged. As his eyes adjusted to the gloom, he picked out a few motionless heaps.

He scuttled up to the first lump and saw it was Taggert, one of the youngest guys in his A-team. He checked for a pulse. Nothing. With a gentle tap, he rolled Taggert onto his back to reveal wide, unseeing eyes. A gaping hole was where his chest should be. Like a goddamn cannon ball.

He choked back the bile. He'd failed Taggert.

He turned and saw another heap close by and half crawled over, fearing the worst. His breath came in unsteady bursts now. His stomach roped into knots so tight he couldn't believe he was breathing at all.

Still silence reigned.

Smoke billowed.

The doorway was no longer empty. A handful of bearded men poured out, their mouths open, assault rifles brandished, and gazes sweeping around quickly. How the hell could they not be making any noise?

He flopped down next to his other soldier and played possum. He slowed his breath and stiffened every muscle. Shifted his eyes to the side.

He screamed.

He screamed, yet nothing came out. His throat was blocked, as if a pile of bricks had obstructed his windpipe.

All that remained was a face blown clean apart.

Hands grabbed his arms and legs. Four men. No, was it five? Picked him up, mouths wide as if screaming at him, but still he remained deaf to their cries. They carted him in through the doorway, despite his struggles.

"Nooooooooo!" The scream rang in his head. "Noooo."

His eyes flew open. Salty sweat dripped in his eyes, but he was in his garage, hanging from his pull-up bar, not captured in Iraq. Now he was dreaming awake? What the hell?

Only twenty more reps to go. No excuses. No wimping out. Every muscle in his body screamed as he jerked himself up to the bar. Physical pain beat the waking nightmares any day.

"Christian?" His buddy Brandt's voice infiltrated his haze. Seven. Six…

"Dude, you trying to kill yourself?"

"Four, three, two, one." He dropped to the garage floor and grabbed his towel. Scrubbed the sweat from his face. "Just finishing up, that's all."

"I've been standing here for five minutes, and you look like you're vying for a role in a reboot of

Terminator. How many of those things you do anyway?" Brandt's tone was light, but his blue eyes were narrowed.

"Don't worry about it. Got to keep in shape." He grunted and walked past his buddy toward the door into the house.

"Okaaayyy. Running Vines must be more challenging than I thought," Brandt cracked as he followed him into the house.

Christian trudged to the refrigerator and yanked out a bottle of water. He rubbed it across his steaming forehead before sucking down half of it in one gulp.

"So you're in one of your chatty moods today? Should I just call you later?"

"What?" He worked to slow down his breath and smiled when Olive galloped toward him as if he'd been gone for months instead of in the garage for an hour. She held up her front paws, and he picked her up.

"What the hell is *that?* A mutant rat?" Brandt's voice raised an octave.

"Hey, man, don't hate on my dog. This is Olive." He angled her cute face toward his friend. "Apologize to her."

"Or what? You'll make me do pull-ups?" Brandt laughed. "When did you get a rat? I mean, dog?" He held his hands up to ward off Christian's glare.

"When I went up to Pups-4-Vets yesterday. We just kind of clicked." More like the dog glued herself to him until he couldn't deny she was awesome.

"Pups-4-Vets? Is that the place Kelly was talking about? Aren't those dogs for disabled soldiers?" Brandt's smile faded away as his dark brows arched.

Shit. Shit. Shit. He wasn't a liar. Although he'd

shared some of his PTS issue with Nick, he hadn't confided in Brandt. But maybe part of resolving his shit was owning his posttraumatic stress, owning the waking nightmare he'd just endured.

"Yeah, turns out pugs are great dogs for anxiety and panic attacks." He kept his back to Brandt, unwilling to see his reaction.

"Dude, from the war?" Brandt's voice was sober.

"Yeah, nightmares, anxiety. It's a laugh a minute. Part of why I resigned my commission early—hell, it's mostly why I came back. Why I'm trying to live a normal civilian life without all the stress." He'd turned and leaned against the counter, Olive cradled in his arms. Who cared what it looked like? He loved the damn dog.

"I'm sorry. I would never have guessed. Well, if the furry thing calms you down, I guess it doesn't matter how fugly she is." Brandt laughed, and just like that, the tension gripping Christian's shoulders eased.

"Yeah, who would've thought?" He gazed down at Olive and scratched between her lopsided ears. "So what's up?"

"Well, a couple things. You know Alyssa and I are getting married, and I wanted to see if you'd be a groomsman."

"Wow, yeah. Can't believe you and Nick's baby sister, but I knew something was up when I saw you two at the Pageant of the Masters. You were twitchy." Alyssa and Brandt had looked like two kids caught skipping school when he'd run into them one night before they'd revealed their secret love affair.

"Yeah. Well?"

"Of course, of course. Whatever you need." His

two best buddies married and in love. If anyone had told him that when he'd returned to Laguna, he'd have laughed until he'd broken a rib.

"And one more little favor?"

"Yeah?"

"The wine for the reception—can you provide it for us?"

"Sure. Once you figure out how many guests and what flavors you want, I'll get you a deal." Another benefit of the wine bar—wholesale on some amazing bottles.

"Thanks, bro. So Kelly, huh? You seeing her or what?"

He stiffened. When he'd had the panic attack, she'd fawned all over him, as if he were an injured kitten. He'd seen the pity in her eyes. No, he wasn't doing anything at all with Kelly Prescott.

"Nah, just went with her up to the dog place." And been blown away by her beauty, brains, and soft heart. But he wasn't a rescue.

"She's pretty cool, so why wouldn't you date her?"

"Look, just because you and Nick are tying yourselves down doesn't mean I'm ready to join your sewing circle. Just not interested." He ruthlessly squashed down the image of her face after he'd kissed her the first time—swollen pink lips, flushed skin, and glazed caramel eyes.

"Huh. Whatever. Probably better anyway since she's so tight with Sophie and Alyssa. Could be awkward." Brandt nodded, as if agreeing with Christian's silent vow to stay away from Kelly. "Gotta run. Thanks, man." He wheeled around and exited the house.

Christian stared down at Olive, who'd snuggled into the crook of his arm. For the foreseeable future, she was the sole female in his life.

****

"Come in." Kelly lifted her head from the love seat where she was sprawled. She'd called Sophie after about an hour of staring at the ceiling, and not in a meditative kind of way.

"Hey, sweetie, are you okay?" Sophie plopped down on the cushion next to her. Thank goodness for best friends.

"I'll be fine. Just trying to process all of it. One minute we're sharing a mind-blowing kiss in the middle of the hiking trail, and then the earthquake started, and he slams us to the ground."

"Hold on one second. Mind-blowing kiss on the hiking trail? Was that your first kiss?" Sophie's big blue eyes widened.

"Well, I told you he went with me to Pups-4-Vets and adopted Olive—she is such a cutie-pie." She shrugged self-consciously. "I may have failed to mention we kissed yesterday at his house." And the kiss had the potential to be the start of something. Well, something passionate at least.

"Keeping secrets? So one kiss led to a hike to another kiss? Details please?" Sophie waggled her eyebrows.

"Yesterday was like something out of a steamy romance novel...best kiss ever. Like all the stuff about still waters running deep." She smiled despite herself. "Today was more of an accident. I tripped—"

"Ha. The legendary Clumsy Kelly showed up?" Sophie loved to tease her about what an utter klutz she was. And it was true.

"Do you want to hear what happened or not?" She huffed out a breath. It wasn't her fault grace wasn't her middle name.

"Sorry. I know you're upset. I'm not trying to make light of it." Sophie's grin faded.

"There was a gigantic root and it jumped out to attack my foot and I was on course for a face plant and he caught me. And pulled me back against his rock hard—"

"Rock hard…" Sophie hooted.

"Chest. His rock-hard chest. Sculpted pecs. And abs. And…anyway, he nibbled on my neck and boom…fireworks. Then the earthquake hit, and he hauled me to the ground." She shook her head. "Afterward, his eyes were blank, you know?" She rubbed her hands on her chilled arms.

"So Olive is comforting him, and we decide to head back. I can tell he feels awful—he was all sweaty and pale. I couldn't stop myself. I kept asking what I could do. I just wanted to help him feel better." She gripped her hands together.

"Of course you did. Anyone would. Go on." Sophie nodded.

"Well, he snapped at me and told me he didn't want to see me anymore." She shuddered remembering his flat, toneless voice.

"Had he said he wanted to date you?"

"Yeah, after we came back from Pups-4-Vets. We really clicked and celebrated Olive with wine and pizza. And that kiss…" She sighed. It had felt so natural to be in his arms. Not that she'd been picking out china patterns, but the chemistry between them had nearly set his kitchen alight.

"Maybe he was embarrassed?" Sophie's brow furrowed.

"Probably. This is between us, but Christian admitted yesterday at Pups-4-Vets he suffered from PTS. Olive latched onto him, and I think he fell head over heels for her. Melinda, the director, said Olive could only go to a service member with documented posttraumatic stress issues. He admitted he had anxiety, panic attacks, and nightmares. Does Nick know?" How deep did his issues go?

Sophie shook her head. "Christian's pretty private, and you know how guys are. I'm sure he, Nick, and Brandt didn't exactly have a slumber party and share their darkest secrets."

"Probably not. Anyway, I have no idea how serious it is. He obviously wanted the dog bad enough to admit it. And the earthquake must have triggered an episode. I felt terrible." She pushed off the couch and paced around the living room.

"I hope he's feeling better. But you know how you always have the best advice for me?"

"Yes." She bit her lip, knowing what was coming.

"You know your tendencies to nurse the wounded birds back to health, right?"

She nodded. Oh yes, her issues trying to fight her brother's battle with drugs ran deep. She was the one who adopted anything or anyone who needed mending. She'd managed to avoid her patterns in romantic relationships—Robert definitely hadn't required caretaking. Her predisposition to gravitate to those needing help hadn't disappeared, however.

"Well, you know you can't save people, right? You

deserve a guy who can be your equal. Not someone who could be if only…" Sophie trailed off. "Maybe his PTS isn't severe, but it's obviously a factor to consider."

"I know, I know. But he seems fine in every other way. His business is thriving. His home is really neat." The order of his shelves made her scalp tingle in excitement.

"*Neat*? Like neat and tidy? Come on, Kelly, really?" Sophie's eyebrows flew up to her hairline.

"Well, I was quite thrilled at the organization, to be honest." She grinned self-deprecatingly. "All I mean is he seems really together. Except for today."

"Exactly. Even if Olive is a miracle dog, there's no guarantee he's recovered. And you don't know him well enough to know if there are worse incidents. You said he had nightmares, right?"

Kelly bit her lip again. Sophie was right. The smart thing to do would be to just forget about him. Relegate him back to the hot wine-bar owner.

"You're probably right. But I just have this feeling about him…" Deeper than an initial spark. And not because he was wounded and she was a nurturer. He was strong, smart, loyal, caring—she'd seen it.

"Kelly, you just got to Laguna. You're now working in nonprofit with tons of worthy people to nurture. They won't suck out all your energy, like your brother's situation did. Just step back at least. I hate to see you get hurt." Sophie joined her by the huge picture window to share the beautiful view of the Pacific.

"You're right. And he's made it clear he doesn't want to see me, so I guess it is a moot point." She swallowed down the disappointment.

"It'll be okay. It was just a few kisses." Sophie rubbed her shoulder.

"Like you didn't know with Nick after your first kiss." Nick and Sophie's whirlwind romance happened right after Sophie had been jilted at the altar in San Diego and moved to Laguna.

Sophie turned to her. "Wow. Listen to me. You're totally right. Tables are turned, I guess. You were the voice of reason. I just love you and can't help being protective after all the crap with the firm and Robert. Just go slow, okay?"

"Yeah. What are you up to for the rest of the afternoon? Beach walk? My hike did get cut short after all." She laughed—either laugh or cry, right?

"Sure. I'll run home and get changed and be back in fifteen. Deal?" Sophie bolted out the door.

Kelly dropped onto the couch and hugged her knees into her chest. Squeezing her eyes shut, she summoned her resolve to focus on her new career and pour not just her intellect and work ethic into Peaceful Warrior but her whole heart. At the Prescott Firm, she'd been forced to operate with her head and keep her emotions separate. Corporate attorneys didn't bill hundreds of dollars per hour to be kind. Now she would be somewhere her empathy and compassion were valued. She'd channel her passion for helping the disenfranchised to every single veteran she encountered.

Except for Christian Wolfe.

Chapter 14

Kelly hung up the office phone with a decisive click. One more meeting scheduled with prior legal counsel to debrief on the cases they'd handled for Peaceful Warrior. She'd made it to the bottom of her initial to-do list. She'd worked from seven a.m. to seven p.m. for days, fulfilling her promise to herself to bury herself in work. If specters of a certain gorgeous wine bar owner popped into her brain, she ruthlessly crushed them.

Someone knocked briskly on her office door.

"Come in," she called, assuming it was either Mr. Williams or Susan because she didn't have any appointments on the calendar.

Susan poked her head around the door. "Do you by any chance have a few minutes to talk to one of our regulars? He really needs some help, doesn't have a phone, and just showed up."

Again, this scenario never occurred back at the Prescott Firm. No, her secretary would book her calendar, and everything was scheduled to the minute— billable hours and such.

"Sure. Let me just close out this project, and you can send him in. Give me two minutes." Actually, she welcomed the chance to meet one of the clients.

A slight man with dark blond hair in a high and tight, a camouflage jacket, and a pronounced limp entered her office. He nodded at her and headed to one of the two battered office chairs sitting in front of her desk.

"Thanks for seeing me, ma'am. Name's Kyle Warren." He kept nodding and stood in front of the chair, as if he were awaiting orders.

"Please have a seat, Mr. Warren. What can I do for you?" She smiled and leaned forward in her seat.

"Well ma'am..." He paused, swallowing so hard his Adam's apple bobbed in his pencil-thin throat. "I've been having some trouble with my landlord and I'm afraid he'll be evicting me and I've got nowhere to go." He stared down at his trembling hands as if they contained the secrets of the universe.

"I'm sure I can help you with it." Crap, she'd never handled landlord-tenant law, but she knew how to research. "Can you give me more details? Is he harassing you or discriminating against you?"

"Well, I've been a little late on my rent..." He kept his gaze glued on his lap.

"Are you having financial trouble? I'm sure if there's a good reason, I can bargain with your landlord for some extra time." Why wouldn't the landlord give this guy a break?

He lifted bleak bloodshot eyes at her. "I can't get in trouble for what I tell you?"

Uh-oh. A twinge of warning shot up her spine. "Of course, we have attorney-client privilege. You can tell me anything. What's going on?"

"Well, I'm in frightful pain with my leg—the bottom half got blown clear off in Afghanistan—and so the doctor, he gave me some pain pills. Insurance kinda stinks, and so I've been having to pay out of pocket cuz

I can't sleep without them, and my disability checks don't cover it all…"

"What kind of pain pills?" Oh no.

When he shared he was taking the strongest narcotics on the market and paying close to nine hundred dollars a month for them, her heart clutched. Peter had been hooked on those pills before he overdosed. They were some of the most addictive medicine on the market. Manufactured by Hexaun, of course. Damn it. Could she never escape their reach?

"Is there a reason insurance isn't covering these? Why you are paying out of pocket?" She kept her tone gentle, but her neck and shoulders clenched.

He shrugged his narrow shoulders. "They just won't. And there's no generic. Nothing else works. I feel like I'm gonna die when I don't take 'em."

"How short are you on rent and when is it due?" Damn expensive, addictive drugs.

"Well, it's due by next week, and this is the third time I've been late. He said this was it. Not on time, then I'm out. But I'm five hundred dollars short and don't have another check coming until next month."

"Could you borrow any money from your family?"

"No way. They got less than me. I'm afraid I'm going to end up on the street." He was shaking.

Damn. Damn. Damn. No, this poor man would not end up on the street. "Kyle, let me make some phone calls and check some things for you. Can you give me your landlord's name and information?"

He nodded, a glint of hope sparking in his watery eyes.

"Let me work on it this afternoon. We'll find a resolution. Check back with Susan in the next day or two." She'd figure out something to help him.

"Yes, ma'am. Thank you so much. Thank you." He shuffled out of the office.

When the door closed, she dropped her forehead onto the desk and thunked it a few times on the solid oak. What were the odds the first veteran she met was addicted to pain pills and losing all his money paying for them? Flashbacks to Peter's tragic demise assaulted her.

Her brother had been three years older than her. They'd been close, bonding with each other as neither of their parents bothered to be around. They'd attended private school—only the best for the Prescotts.

In college, Peter's unhappiness could no longer be hidden. Many of the other kids also had a lot of pressure at home, and rebelling by getting high was a natural extension of thumbing their noses at their parents. Unfortunately for Peter, he'd gotten hooked, caught, punished, and sent to a fancy rehab facility. But it was too late. Drugs had sunk their fangs into him and refused to release him.

Despite Peter's unexemplary grades, her father pulled strings and he'd gotten into law school. Someone had to carry on the Prescott legacy. While she battled to save him, nothing she did could exorcise his demons. He'd overdosed on a combination of sleeping pills and pain pills. In the end, nothing could numb his pain.

Would she ever recover from losing him?

Her phone rang, and she heaved a sigh of relief when Sophie's name appeared on the screen.

"Hi."

"What's the matter? Are you okay?" Sophie's voice deepened with concern.

"Not really." Her voice cracked. Although it had been years since Peter's death, today it felt like yesterday.

"Did your dad do something? What happened?"

"No, haven't heard a word from him. It's just a client came in and..." Her voice broke again, and she blinked back tears.

"Kelly?"

"A client came in, and well, I can't go into details with you, but it involves the same drugs Peter OD'd on." She paused and smoothed back her hair. "It just brings it all back. I want to help this guy."

"Of course you want to help. It's why you're there. You'll always love and miss your brother. It's not your fault. Anything I can do to help?"

"No, I need to dig in and see what I can do. I don't know if we have any kind of loan program or extra housing assistance. I can't let this guy get dumped out on the streets." She tapped her pen on the desk.

"You'll find a solution. Try and separate your emotions and keep your lawyer hat on."

"You're right. I'll jam the hat on tight. Thanks for listening. What's up with you?" She'd succeeded in keeping her personal life separate from her business life, and she'd continue to do so.

"I feel frivolous switching to something like this, but Alyssa and Brandt decided to throw an informal engagement party."

"Oh great. I'd love to go. When is it? In the next few months?" She'd feel normal by then, wouldn't she?

"Um, try Saturday night."

"This Saturday? In five days? Seriously?" Who held an engagement party with less than a week's notice?

"Well, Vines has an awesome back room that's usually booked out a year in advance. There was a cancellation and Christian just happened to mention it to Brandt and he decided to hop on it because Alyssa was getting a little crazy with the planning of it as well as the wedding." Sophie's words poured out in a rush.

"Vines?" Her stomach plummeted. Seriously? Weren't there any other venues in Laguna besides Christian's?

"Yeah. It's okay, right? Has he called or anything?" Sophie's tone turned cautious.

"Nope. Not awkward at all. Ha. Seriously, it's fine. What time? And do you need me to help?" She and Sophie were bridesmaids, so skipping it because she wasn't ready to see Christian wasn't an option.

"Alyssa and Brandt have it handled. Casual— cocktails and hors d'oeuvres. Semiformal, so wear a smoking-hot outfit. Even if dating him isn't a great idea, you can remind him what he's missing."

"Do you think he's missing me?" She'd been unable to keep him out of her mind since they'd last seen each other. Despite focusing on work, working out, and reading a few juicy novels until she exhausted herself enough to sleep.

"Well, I haven't talked to him, but you're fabulous and amazing, so he'd have to be crazy not to be, right?"

"Ha. And that's why you're my best friend." If only she felt as confident in her personal life as in her professional one.

"Do you want to go with Nick and me?"

"Maybe. I may just meet you there, you know, make an appearance. That way if it's awkward with

Christian, I can bail." How could it not be awkward?

After they hung up, she stood and stalked to her tiny window, savoring the hint of sunshine filtering in through the tree branches. She pressed her palm against the cool, smooth windowpane and inhaled a cleansing breath. She shook off the memories of her brother Peter—he was gone. She'd direct her energy into helping Kyle Warren and fulfill her purpose as general counsel. Daydreams of the tall, dark, and unavailable Mr. Wolfe could wait. Memories of his passionate kisses tended to surface when she laid her head down on the pillow.

Just as they had haunted her every night this week.

Chapter 15

Christian double-checked Vines' back room for the tenth time. Sparkling champagne flutes were lined up like soldiers in formation, awaiting orders to tilt bottoms up. The private event space mirrored the rest of the wine bar with high wood-beamed ceilings, polished mahogany tables, and leather barstools, with the addition of forest-green love seats and comfortable chairs. Platters of charcuterie and plump cheeses sat next to dishes of glistening olives and crisp sliced baguettes. Gorgeous jumbo shrimp and trays of fresh bruschetta decorated the large buffet tables. Lively guitar music flowed out from the speakers cleverly concealed in the exposed brick walls. Perfect. He surveyed the room one more time and turned to return to his office.

"Am I the first one here?" a familiar husky voice inquired.

He froze and barely managed to keep his tongue from hanging out of his mouth.

"Hello?" Kelly tilted her beautiful golden head and arched a brow when he simply stared.

"Hi." Shit. Back to acting like a monosyllabic idiot. Her delectable body was highlighted in a tiny sparkly dress cut down dangerously low and hemmed dangerously high. Her silky golden skin beckoned to him, and he was instantly aroused.

She looked around the room, and the silence hung heavy. Damn it, couldn't he man up?

"I just opened a bottle of champagne. Let me get you a glass." *And get my shit together*. He pivoted away from her and forced himself not to sprint to the buffet table where champagne was chilling in buckets. He grabbed the open bottle and offered a prayer of thanks for the icy exterior. He'd started to sweat.

Her scent greeted him, signaling she'd followed him across the room. Tonight her usual cinnamon scent was amplified, more exotic and lush, tempting him to taste. He filled a flute for her, and miraculously, he managed not to spill any of the crisp liquid. He handed the glass to her, and their fingers brushed, singeing him. They both jolted, the cold liquid splashing their fingers. He'd kept his head lowered, unwilling to meet her gaze, and caught a glimpse of sky-high stilettos and slick red toenails.

Dangerous. He jerked his gaze to her face. Even more perilous. Her full lips were painted scarlet too. Her long sun-streaked hair was sleek and straight, emphasizing her killer cheekbones and exotic cat eyes.

"So…" His mind was blank. All he wanted was to lean over and lick her like an ice cream cone. A delicious salted caramel.

"So." She tasted her champagne and gazed at him over the rim of the glass. Her eyes were unreadable, the usual warmth and laughter absent. Was this her lawyer mode?

"Look, Kelly, I owe you an apology. I was a total jerk…"

She simply nodded and took another sip of champagne. So she wasn't going to make it easy on him.

"The earthquake triggered one of my headaches. I just needed to get home. It wasn't personal." He'd hated her witnessing his meltdown.

"Not personal?" A hint of anger laced her usually rich whisky voice. "I don't think so. You were crystal clear when you told me you didn't want to see me again."

"Well." Lawyer mode was magnificent, scary but magnificent. His hands itched to grasp her shoulders and yank her into his body. Kiss her tempting mouth and run his hands down her spine. He curled his fingers into fists.

"Well what? We're adults. I know it was intense, but I was only trying to help. So either you want to date me or you don't. It's a yes or no question." She sounded incredibly confident, but her hand shook a little as she defiantly drained her glass.

"Yes or no?" Every muscle in his body stiffened.

"Yes or no. It's simple." She placed both hands on her slender hips and glared at him.

"It's not so simple, I—" *I want to tear off your dress and take you up against the wall. I want to bury myself inside you. I want you.*

"Christian, Kelly—hi." Alyssa sailed into the room, interrupting his response. She kissed Christian on the cheek first and then hugged Kelly.

The moment was lost.

"Christian, it looks incredible in here. Thank you so much." Alyssa beamed as she took in the spread.

"Happy it all worked out. Where's Brandt?" *Act cool.*

"He's in the restroom. I need champagne. Come

126

on, Kel. It looks like you started without me." Alyssa threaded her arm through Kelly's and strolled over to the tables. Kelly didn't glance back.

It was probably for the best.

People flooded into the room, and no opportunity to be alone with her arose. Because Brandt was one of his closest friends, Christian personally oversaw the party. Sure. It was definitely the only reason he stayed. Not to stare at Kelly or anything.

He couldn't tear his eyes off her. She'd been cozying up with some smooth corporate guy he didn't recognize. She laughed and flirted as if she didn't have a care in the world. As if she hadn't just challenged him to admit he wanted her. The guy stroked a manicured pale hand down her sleek shoulder, and he took one step toward them before he caught himself. He had no right to her. She was better off with someone who didn't have enough baggage to set sail around the world for eighty days. She deserved better than him.

But seeing her this way, close yet out of reach, struck something inside his chest. Damn it, when did he become a coward? He'd earned numerous medals for bravery, but midnight missions and dodging bombs seemed easy compared to figuring out what to do about Kelly Prescott. She was so strong and beautiful. Damn it, the answer was *yes*. Yes, he wanted to see her. Every delicious inch of her.

Alyssa appeared at his side. "What's the grimace for?"

"I'm not grimacing. Just thinking." Yeah, right. He was just thinking.

"Okay, of course you are. Thinking pretty hard in Kelly's direction." She chuckled. "But I came over to say thanks. The party is perfect, and we're so grateful you offered us the room." She kissed his cheek.

"Glad to help." Alyssa and Brandt were two of his favorite people.

"So why are you glaring at Kelly instead of hanging out with her?" Her tone turned teasing.

"Huh?" Maybe he didn't like her so much after all.

"Don't play dumb with me. You two have been staring at each other all night. Sophie and I call it 'googly eyes.' Why don't you just ask her out? You're single, right?" Alyssa pinned him with her sharp gaze.

"*Googly eyes*? Are you serious?" What the hell?

"Sophie told me about when Kelly came up to visit her the first time and came in with Nick. You two were making googly eyes at each other." She winked one eye and pursed her lips.

"I've got to go—" He turned away to escape the line of questioning. *Googly eyes, my ass.*

"Christian.*"* She grasped his arm, halting his progress. "Sorry, I don't mean to pry, but you two both can't keep your eyes off each other, but it's obvious you're avoiding each other—"

"Obvious?" He scanned the room, half expecting everyone to be staring at him. Nobody was.

He hated being the center of attention.

"Well, to those of us who know both of you. Yes." She nodded vigorously.

"Huh." His usually robust vocabulary deserted him. Again.

"Just go talk to her." She squeezed his arm before flitting off.

He looked at Kelly—of course he knew exactly where she was in the room—and her honey gaze snared him.

Something unfamiliar stirred in his gut. He started toward her and then halted. No, damn it, he couldn't chance it. He desired her more than he'd ever wanted a woman, but she deserved more.

He pivoted and retreated from the private room back to the safety of his office.

****

Are you kidding me? His shimmering eyes captured hers from across the room, and heat shot straight to her center. They'd evaded each other all night, but every time she looked up, she'd caught him watching her. Her senses betrayed her, attuned to his every move, as if she were a homing pigeon.

He took a step toward her, and her spine stiffened. She braced for another encounter. Then he turned on his heel and high-tailed it out of the room. Ludicrous.

She huffed out an exasperated breath. Enough was enough. If he were too much of a chicken to act like an adult, she'd lead the charge. She would march into his office and demand they clear the air and end this awkward dance. They had a connection, a kind of recognition when their eyes first met last year. Hell, she and Sophie experienced the same reaction when they'd met as kids. Sometimes you click.

Enough was enough. She'd go batty without some type of resolution. Was he in or out? She squared her shoulders and marched into the wine bar's main room, pausing to admire what he'd created with his vision. Conversations buzzed, and glasses clinked. The soaring ceilings created an open ambiance, and the exposed brick wall and floor-to-ceiling windows invited in the crisp breeze.

Where was he?

Maybe he'd left? Or was he in his office?

She skirted the bar and waved at Amy, the waitress she'd met a few times with Sophie, and rapped on his office door. Without waiting for a reply, she stepped onto the lush burgundy carpet. He sat behind a giant desk, engrossed in whatever lit up his computer screen.

Before she could utter a word, his head popped up and he pierced her with those unusual green-gold eyes.

Her mind blanked. What was she going to say again?

"Kelly, did you need something?" Back to formal politeness. Lovely.

"Yes, I want to finish our conversation." *Here goes nothing.* She closed the door and flipped the lock with a decisive click. Inhaling deeply, she sauntered into the room on now-shaky legs, her stilettos sinking into the luxurious rug.

He simply stared, his square jaw set, his expression remote. Damn him.

"Christian?" She froze, ready to flee from this taciturn man.

"Wait." His quiet voice stopped her.

He rose from the chair and stalked toward her, the silent stranger morphing into a tiger tracking its prey. Her mouth fell open. He stopped in front of her and grasped her shoulders.

The office surroundings melted away. The buzz of the bar faded in the distance. Only the beautiful man remained. Her skin heated from his large firm hands on her bare flesh. Flames raced directly to her center. His crisp masculine scent enveloped her.

With a groan, he hauled her against him, and his

dark head descended to capture her lips. Her breasts were crushed against the solid wall of his chest, and she wound her arms around his neck, thrusting her fingers into his thick silky hair. He stroked her tongue with his, and their breaths mingled. Hints of wine and something darker and more delicious assaulted her. His powerful thigh pressed between her legs, and she rocked her center against him.

"You're so beautiful. So perfect." He nibbled along her neck, his lips trailing down to her collarbone and moving lower. One hand captured her breast, and he brushed his thumb against her aching, aroused nipple.

Her head dropped back, and she arched against him. Pleasure surged from her breast straight down to where his leg pressed against her most sensitive spot. When he grazed her nipple with his teeth, she moaned. "Please."

"Please what, beautiful? What do you want?" he whispered against her oversensitive skin.

"More. Please more." Anything. Everything. Whatever he would give her.

With a growl, he slid to the floor, yanking her down next to him. His mouth fastened onto her breast and pulled hard. Sensation shot down to her toes. One hand cupped her bottom and slid her silky dress up, baring her skin. His hand caressed her hip and slipped between her legs. She bucked at the contact, wild for more.

He obliged. He stroked one long finger along her silk underwear and groaned again when he encountered the dampness. "Kelly, you're so sweet."

He recaptured her mouth, and her vision began to blur. He continued stroking against her panties and then tugged them aside. He spread her apart, one finger diving inside her, then two. When his thumb circled her center, she cried against his lips, pleasure flashing through her veins.

"Yes, oh yes, that's it. Let me take care of you." He maintained his sensual assault and pressed the heel of his hand against her sensitized flesh. Pressure built, and tremors escalated through her limbs as she rode his hand, desperate to reach the summit he promised her.

Her eyes closed in ecstasy. His hand stilled, and she moaned in protest. *No*, not yet, not when she was so close.

"Look at me. I want to see you fall apart." His husky voice was demanding, masterful.

She managed to lift her heavy eyelids and his eyes bored into her. His feral smile revealed straight white teeth. "Now. Let go now."

He increased his pace. Unable to hold back another second, she exploded against his hand, rocking her hips. A kaleidoscope of lights burst behind her eyelids. He growled and bit the sensitive spot on her neck, holding on while the shudders shot from her center outwards to every inch of her body. His firm lips pressed featherlight kisses against her neck and then captured her mouth.

He held onto her and stroked one hand down her back until her body stopped vibrating. Slow, lazy kisses continued.

A knock on the door startled them, and they leapt apart like two guilty children caught shaking Christmas presents under the tree. What was she doing on the floor with her dress up around her waist and feeling the most satisfied she'd ever been in her life? Christian offered a hand—heat rose in her cheeks because, wow, what his hand could do—and helped her stand.

"Yeah, what is it?" His voice was husky. He ran his fingers through his thick dark hair and smiled at her.

"Alyssa and Brandt are looking for you—something about a toast?" Amy called through the door.

"I'll be out in a sec," Christian called.

Kelly smoothed her dress down with an unsteady hand. Where was her purse? She could only imagine how disheveled she looked after *that*. Her legs wobbled as she walked over to her evening clutch that had somehow landed halfway under Christian's desk.

"Kelly." He captured both of her hands in his warm ones. He threaded those talented fingers through hers and tugged her closer. He pressed a tender kiss to her lips.

"How about dinner tomorrow night?" He smiled again, his eyes molten pools of gold-flecked green.

"Is the answer yes, then?" She squeezed their interlaced fingers and returned his smile.

"Simple answer to a simple question. Yes. Absolutely yes." He released her hands. "I'll call you. Come on. We can't miss the toasts."

"Let me comb my hair and put on some lipstick first." Who knew what she looked like? A cat that swallowed the cream, perhaps? A delicious laziness permeated her body.

"You look beautiful all mussed up, but you're probably right." He waited while she hastily smoothed down her disheveled hair and reapplied more scarlet lipstick to her bare, thoroughly kissed lips.

She squared her shoulders and sauntered back to the party with him. He plucked two fresh flutes of champagne from a passing waiter's tray, and they toasted Alyssa and Brandt. Kelly's tingling lips refused to stop smiling.

What would tomorrow night bring?

Chapter 16

Christian tossed the razor onto the bathroom countertop and splashed icy water on his freshly shaved face. The mirror didn't expose his trepidation, but his heartbeat raced as if he were the high school nerd escorting the homecoming queen to the prom. Suspicious of how he'd gotten so lucky and terrified he'd screw it up.

He'd created a rocking new playlist because he knew she appreciated the same powerful music. Selected a special bottle of merlot from his private collection. He'd changed the sheets on his bed. Triple-checked everything in the house was in perfect order. Just in case.

Just in case Kelly came home with him after dinner.

God, please let her come home with him after dinner.

Not that he expected sex or anything, although he had bought a new jumbo box of condoms.

Just in case.

He was getting ahead of himself. Despite the nerves, he wanted to spend more time with her. Period. Take it slow. After the hike ended in the earthquake debacle, he'd sworn he'd stay away from her. But he couldn't. Not just because he kept tasting her kiss on his lips. No, her intellect and strength intrigued him. He wouldn't plan ahead. He'd just see what happened.

He buttoned up his midnight-blue dress shirt and tucked it into a pair of dark jeans. Evening wear, Southern California style. He grabbed a peanut-butter crunchy treat for Olive out of the ceramic jar on the counter.

"What do you think, girl? Am I ready for a date? Bark once for yes and twice for no." Damn, he was pathetic.

Olive remained curled in her red dog bed and tilted her head in consideration. He scratched her lopsided ears and grinned. This fur ball filled him with joy.

"C'mon, Olive. Help me out." Could she sense his nerves? He hadn't had a woman over since he'd returned from the Middle East. His nightmares could be violent. Over the last few years, he'd punched a hole in his bedroom wall, knocked a lamp off his bedside table, and woken up curled up in a ball on the floor. And his Buzz Lightyear nightlight wasn't exactly an aphrodisiac.

"Woof." Did her head actually nod in approval?

"Thanks, girl. See you later." Two-sided conversations with a ten-pound beast—he'd officially lost it.

He grabbed the keys to his jeep, a bottle of Paso Robles red wine, and the bouquet of sunflowers he'd bought, and he sauntered to his car. Now or never.

When he arrived at her house, the nerd toting a bouquet of flowers instead of a corsage of colored carnations, he squared his shoulders and knocked. She opened the door, and his mind blanked. Every inch of him jumped to attention. Holy hell.

She wore white lace, but her dress and open-toed

stilettos were anything but innocent. Her sun-streaked hair cascaded in beachy waves; the dress was high necked, but somehow her shoulders and arms were bare, showcasing her silky golden skin. The skirt stopped midthigh, and her shoes had some type of ankle strap that made him want to untie them with his teeth. And continue kissing up her toned calves and taut thighs to her—

"Christian?" Her plump lips curved into a smile. "Are those for me?"

"Of course, they remind me of you, all golden." *Drag your jaw up off the floor, man.*

"Um, do you want to give them to me?" Her eyes crinkled at the corners as her grin deepened.

"Here." Damn. Shaking his head, he forced himself to step forward and thrust the flowers into her hands.

"Thanks. Come on in." Her slender fingers brushed his, and rosy color flooded her cheeks. Did the hue travel further down her body when she was turned on?

Focus. "I brought my one of my favorite wines. Want to have a glass before we head to Marino's?" *Talk, be friendly, act normal.*

"I'd love to. Let me put these in a vase, and let's open it up." She strolled to the kitchen.

He clenched his teeth together to prevent drooling. What was it about the contrast of the lace dress and those white ribbons circling her ankles? He ripped his gaze higher, but her dress highlighted her toned, tanned back. He swallowed.

She whirled to face him and handed him two glasses and the wine opener. Sweat popped up on his brow when her short skirt fluttered around her legs. He glued his eyes to the task of opening the bottle while she arranged the flowers in a metallic brass vase.

Open bottle. Drink like normal person. Keep eyes on her face.

He grabbed the wineglass and chugged half the liquid in one gulp. Maybe the cool wine would douse his arousal from the inside out. He summoned the latest baseball stats, anything to avoid embarrassing himself.

"Thirsty?" Her husky voice tempted him.

"A little bit, yeah. And the reservation, the reservation is at seven, so we should probably get going. Don't want to be late." Way to act cool. Shit, was he stammering?

"Okay, no problem. Are you okay? You look a little...overheated." Her light brown eyebrows arched over molten-gold cat eyes.

Damn it, he needed to regain his control. "I'm fine. Just don't want to be late." *Because I am ready to take you right here, right now.* If they didn't leave, he might not be able to resist thrusting her against the wall next to the kitchen's pantry, grabbing one of those delectable ankles, shoving up her lace skirt and burying himself to the hilt.

"You know I love punctuality," she teased and picked up a small golden handbag. "Let's do this."

He tossed back the rest of the wine and slammed the glass on the counter. *Nice date, woo her, be a gentleman.* His brain registered the messages, but his body was lagging way behind. Maybe he'd traveled back in time to high school after all.

****

Holy smokes. When Kelly opened her front door, she'd almost liquefied into a puddle on the spot. Christian's dark hair waved across his tanned forehead, his eyes gleamed from the twilight of the porch, and his chiseled features evoked every schoolgirl pirate fantasy she could recall. He'd silently stared at her, like a tiger intent upon devouring his next feast.

She'd worn the sexy yet sweet lace halter minidress and her favorite peekaboo skyscraper heels to tempt him. And judging from his dazed expression, his hurried guzzling of his wine as if he'd just survived days crossing a barren desert, and his dogged insistence they leave, she'd succeeded. It was as if he didn't trust himself not to pounce. Anticipation bubbled through her system.

When they arrived at Marino's, his warm hand seared against her lower back as he escorted her to their secluded corner table. His appealing crisp, clean scent surrounded her when he pushed her chair in for her.

"I've heard about Marino's from Sophie. She says it's Nick's favorite Italian restaurant. Yours too?" Nick had taken Sophie here on their first date. It must be the romantic hot spot of Laguna.

A tuxedo-clad waiter appeared at the table with a bottle of wine. At Christian's nod, the server uncorked it.

"Except for my grandmother's cooking, it's the best Italian. The chef prepares nightly specials. You up for it?"

"Of course." She was up for anything as long as he was involved.

"An order of bruschetta and two specials, thank you, Antonio," Christian told the waiter, who placed the opened bottle onto the table.

Your grandmother? Does she live here?" Kelly leaned forward, eager to learn more about his family.

"Not any more. My parents retired a few years back and moved out to Palm Desert. She went with them. So now I have to get my Italian fix here or try to make it myself." He shrugged and poured wine into her glass.

"Are both your parents Italian?" Did his heritage explain his dark, dangerous good looks?

"No, just on my mom's side. My grandmother came over from Naples when she was still a girl. She's amazing."

"She must love that you have a wine bar now. Has she seen it?"

"Yes, part of my inspiration of opening Vines was from her encouragement." He grinned. "I almost called it Nana's, but she wouldn't let me."

"It's wonderful to have your family encourage your endeavors." She sipped her wine, hoping it would mask the bitter taste she couldn't seem to remove whenever she allowed herself to dwell on her own family. She gripped her wineglass and stemmed the flow of negativity. No way would she ruin Christian's relaxed demeanor by raising the specter of her own relatives. "Do you see them often?"

"Holidays mostly. Once I finished college in San Diego and officer training school, I never really lived here again. My little brother went to college in Florida and never left." He shrugged.

"I didn't know you had a brother. What's his name?" Her belly tensed.

"Riley. He's in med school now, in Miami. We talk now and then, but he's seven years younger. We get along, but don't have much in common because I left for college when he was eleven."

"Oh." She shifted back in her chair and rubbed her suddenly chilled arms. A memory of Peter's sweet innocent face when he'd been eleven flashed in front of her, and she closed her eyes for a moment.

"You okay?" He frowned and set down his glass, then reached across the table and laid his hand down, palm up.

"Yeah, I am." She placed her hand in his, and he wound his strong fingers with hers. "Sorry, but sometimes it feels like yesterday that Peter was a child."

"I should apologize. You must miss your brother every day." He squeezed her hand tighter.

"I do. But that doesn't mean I'm not happy for everyone else who has a normal family."

"If you want to tell me more about Peter, I'm here." He gazed into her eyes.

"Thanks, but I don't right now. My friends are my family now. I'm lucky." Thank God for Sophie.

The waiter arrived with a mouthwatering plate of bruschetta, providing the perfect distraction from further discussion of her brother. She tried to tug her hand free, but he merely smiled and held on.

"So." He caressed her palm with his thumb, and a jolt of electricity sparked from her fingertips to her center.

"So." Holy cow. A featherlight caress of his thumb was all it took to arouse her and make her forget about her screwed-up family.

"You've got to tell me what you think of the bruschetta." He grinned knowingly and released her hand to offer her the plate.

Whew. He didn't touch her again throughout the

outstanding meal of delicate Dover sole on a bed of linguini and capers, but her hand still tingled. Conversation settled into a natural rhythm, but attraction sizzled across the dinner table with each long, hot glance and curve of his sculpted lips.

"Can I interest you in some dessert?"

Kelly managed to tear her eyes away from Christian and focus her attention on the discreet waiter who had materialized next to them.

"No, we've got dessert at home. Just the check please," he answered before she could open her mouth.

"Very well, sir." The tuxedo-clad waiter dashed off.

"Dessert at home?" Her tummy did a slow roll in anticipation.

"Gelato. My favorite flavor. Want to go watch a movie at my place?" His smile deepened, and a lock of his dark hair fell across his forehead as he leaned closer.

"Absolutely." Her nipples pebbled. What would it feel like to have his caress there? His mouth? Forget the watching a movie part... She'd take Christian with a scoop of gelato.

Chapter 17

The ride to his house was a blur, and when they arrived, he made a beeline for the enormous L-shaped couch. He tugged her against him, and a moan hummed up her throat and her vision dimmed. Suddenly, he turned his body and fell backwards onto the cushions and she landed in his lap. His hands stroked down her back and up the sides of her waist, seemingly everywhere at once before they entwined in her hair, holding her head still while he plundered her mouth. She wound her arms around his neck and savored his firm lips against hers. His warm breath mingled with hers, and her mouth opened to accept his tongue stroking against hers. Playing. Devouring. Savoring.

The tanned skin on his neck was smooth under her fingertips, and she stroked her hands down to his broad muscular shoulders. Clung to the solid strength like a drowning woman holding on for her life. Finally, he leaned back and brushed her hair away from her sensitive skin. He cupped her jaw in his firm grip, and his fiery gaze burned into hers. She held her breath.

"I'm going to grab us some water." He released her and stood, wiping his palms on his dark jeans. "Let's breathe for a second."

Her exhale whooshed out, and she adjusted the hem of her skirt with an unsteady hand and smoothed her tangled hair away from her face. She gripped her hands together and squeezed. *My goodness.* What now?

He returned with two glasses of water, looking sexy as hell with his rumpled hair and half-unbuttoned shirt. Had she started undressing him? He sat down next to her and reached for the remote control on the teak coffee table. She accepted the glass he offered and sipped, the ice cubes clinking on the glass. Was he trying to cool them off literally?

"I have to apologize for tossing you onto the couch. I promised you a movie and gelato, not to just bring you home and jump your bones." He slanted his heated gaze at her.

"Christian..." Could she be really forward? His eyes were heavy lidded, his arousal was obvious in his jeans, and what did she have to lose? "I'd rather you jump my bones please."

His eyes narrowed, and he set down his drink with military precision. He took her glass and placed it next to his.

"Are you sure?" He was very still, his eyes deepened to black, with only a sliver of greenish gold remaining. She ran her tongue across her upper lip and stroked her hand up his powerful denim-clad thigh and nodded.

Control snapped. He pounced, scooped her up in his arms, strode into his bedroom, and kicked the door shut behind him. She shivered in anticipation, and he released her so she slid down his body. Every inch of her flesh brushed across the flat planes of his chiseled muscles. His rigid length dug into her belly, and she squeezed her inner muscles.

"The dress. Take it off. Now," he growled against her lips, his raspy voice a sensuous command.

"So you're bossy?" Her toes curled in her stilettos, and a lightning strike of anticipation shot to her core.

"Now, or I'll tear it off." His hands stroked down her exposed back and ran along the seam at the back of her dress. Goose bumps erupted along her bare spine.

"Mmmm…just unzip the skirt, and I'll get the neckline." She reached up to release the button holding up the halter-top bodice of her dress.

His strong hands caressed her hips, stroking and jerking her even closer against his solid length. Cupping her bottom with one hand, he located the zipper and dragged it down. Her dress dropped to the floor.

He held her at arm's length and raked his gaze down her body, clad only in her tiny satin thong. A flush crept across her skin. "Kelly," he whispered. Awe filled his tone. "You are perfect."

"Kiss me." *Take me. Do anything you want to me. Just do it now.*

"Let me worship you, like you deserve." He brushed his lips against hers and then down her neck, pausing to nuzzle the sensitive flesh under her ear. His hands palmed her breasts and his thumbs pinched her nipples, instantly shooting sensation straight to her molten center. Her knees threatened to collapse, but her feet remained glued to the floor. One hand stroked across her belly and cupped her, and her legs buckled.

Somehow the edge of the bed was behind her, and she sank onto the downy mattress. He spread her legs apart, stroking his callused palms up her sensitive inner thighs. He knelt between her legs and with his gaze burning into hers, stroked the inside of her knee with his tongue. Shivers danced across her flesh, and he laughed softly. He lifted one leg, and his lips traveled from her sensitive knee, along her calf, and down to her ankle, where he tugged on the winding straps of her sandals.

"You'll keep these on." He shifted back to the juncture of her thighs and paused. His hands spread her legs further apart, opening her to his gaze. He stroked across her damp panties with a firm thumb. "Damn, you are so beautiful."

"Christian." Her entire body trembled, and perspiration cloaked her skin. "Please."

"Please what?" He looked up at her, a wicked smile on his face.

"Kiss me. Please. Now," she begged. She didn't care. The rest of the world receded, and all that mattered now was he put his mouth on her.

"Since you ask so nicely..." He grinned and lowered his head. He pressed a featherlight kiss along her inner thigh, just inches from her most sensitive spot. Her back bowed off the bed. "Is this where you want me to kiss you?" His hot breath teased her.

"Christian. Please." *Or I might die.*

He yanked her thong off and his tongue stroked along her folds and she arched up to meet him. He gripped her hips, holding her immobile, and tortured her with his lips, his tongue, each kiss deeper and more intense.

The quaking began deep within her and he growled as his fingers dug into her skin and held her in place while she exploded. The orgasm slammed through her, and wave after wave washed over her. He didn't release her until she was still. Once she collapsed on the sheets, he slid up until they were face to face and kissed her.

"You're incredible." Aftershocks of pleasure shot through her body.

"You're incredible." He yanked off his shirt and shucked his jeans. He stood over her, his perfect body glistening with perspiration, ready for her. "Will you let me take charge?"

"Oh my God, yes."

He lowered himself between her legs and poised at her entrance. He slid home in one stroke and they both froze, groaning simultaneously. He filled her to bursting, but her body welcomed the feeling of possession, of his thick, hard length buried inside her. Her inner muscles gripped him. He didn't move for a moment and then shifted to one forearm and smoothed her hair back from her face and stared into her eyes.

"I need to take you hard." His eyes were black, his jaw clenched. "Still okay with letting me?"

"Yes," she moaned.

His gaze remained locked with hers as he took her in powerful strokes, pulling almost all the way out and slamming back into her each time. Forceful. Intense. He grasped her ankles and pressed her knees up by her shoulders. At this angle, he was incredibly deep, but didn't relent on the pace or release her gaze.

Sensation overwhelmed her, and her eyelids floated shut.

"Look at me."

"Yes." She forced her eyes open. His gaze burned into her, holding her prisoner.

"Wrap your legs around me." He released her ankles, and she complied. He reached down and grabbed her bottom and drove deeper. She cried out as the orgasm slammed into her. He covered her mouth with his, but he didn't stop.

He shifted back, flipped her over onto her belly, and dragged her up to her hands and knees. He grasped her hips and drove himself home, thrusting into her with a relentless pace. He leaned over her, one hand grasping her breast and the other stroking her where they were connected.

"I can't. It's too much." Her ears buzzed, her body trembled, and the aftershocks of her last orgasm continued to ripple through her.

"Yes, you can." He stroked deeper, harder, faster than she'd ever experienced. Her hands clawed at the pillows, and she surrendered to his possession. Reveled in it. The slick skin of his chest pressed against her back, his teeth captured the side of her neck, and their mingled moans signaled the simultaneous climax rocking both of them. He collapsed on top of her and then rolled onto his side, remaining inside her, his breath harsh pants against her neck. She reached up to touch her head, making sure it hadn't blown off somewhere during *that*.

After a few minutes, he kissed her and got up and went to the bathroom. She rolled onto her back, every inch of her sated and heavy. Talk about still waters running deep? She'd been thoroughly ravished by a demanding pirate and had loved every minute of it.

He returned, and she wobbled on unsteady legs to the bathroom. She managed to avoid shrieking at her wild lion's mane of hair and swollen red lips. Yes, she looked thoroughly taken care of—no questions there.

When she returned to bed, he pulled her down beside him and they sank into the fluffy pillows. He yanked a cozy blanket around them and snuggled her in close. Her head fit perfectly against his chest, and her lips curved up against his firm pecs when one strong thigh wrapped around hers. He pressed a light kiss against the top of her head, and without a word they drifted off to sleep.

Heaven.

Chapter 18

Acrid smoke assaulted his nostrils, and unbearable heat singed his skin through his uniform. Was he stuck in Hell?

"No! No! Stay back!" He yelled, but no sound seemed to emerge, although his throat felt raw and burned.

Second Lieutenant Mark Murphy from Bozeman, Montana, halted his advance on the gutted ruin of a building, attuned to his commander's order.

The pause cost him his life.

Christian screamed, helpless to do anything from his position behind the chest- high wall blocking him from the city square. He heard the grenade's whizz a split second before it struck Murphy and tossed him to the earth.

He dove and covered his head. Cursed. The air grew silent, and he rose to a crouch and peered around the edge of the barricade. Patrick Dixon, another of his soldiers, shifted out from behind another wall and gestured that the coast was clear. Dixon skirted out before Christian could stop him and edged over to what was left of Murphy to drag him out of the middle of the square.

Just as the soldier reached Murphy, he lurched and fell on top of him.

"No. Damn it. No. What the hell?" Christian's

gaze swung around wildly. Silence. Nobody there. Then a light flickered in a window high atop the closest building. Cursed. Fucking sniper. It'd only been the three of them out there, and now two of his men were dead. Two young, innocent men blown to bits.

He squeezed his eyes shut for a moment. He knew what to do. What he had to do, but he just needed one goddamn minute to catch his breath. He sucked in some air, not caring about the thick, choking dust permeating it. Just a couple of breaths.

A pair of hands slammed down on his shoulders, and he jerked and flipped around to confront the shrouded figure who grabbed him. He threw an elbow, aiming for the attacker's throat.

High-pitched barks pierced the air. Glass broke, and a scream jolted him.

"Christian." A woman's voice. What the hell was a woman doing in his dream? The A-Team was all men.

His eyelids flew open, and he swung his head around. Blinked. He shot up, his skin slick with sweat, his body shaking like a leaf. What the hell? Damn it. The barking increased and frantic scratching on the door reminded him of Olive.

The air was now clear and cool. He ran a trembling hand through his damp hair. He'd sweated more than a bloated tourist sightseeing in New Orleans. What the hell? His throat was clogged with sand, like the desert of his nightmares.

"Christian."

He tracked the voice. He was in his bedroom in Laguna, and Kelly was on the floor, staring up at him with wide eyes.

He flipped on the lamp on his night table to reveal

broken glass surrounding her. The solid glass alarm clock his men had given him as a "retirement" gift when he'd resigned his commission.

"Don't move." He jumped off the other side of the bed and ran to the kitchen to grab a broom and dustpan. He whipped open the door, and Olive immediately ceased her barking.

"It's okay, girl." Damn. Damn. Damn. Despite having the dog, he'd hurt Kelly, just as he feared he would.

He hurried back to his bedroom, sweat trickling down his spine. He flipped on the overhead light and cursed. Damn it, she was bleeding, shivering, and terrified. He switched into military mode and ordered her to stay still once again. He also ordered Olive to stay. Neither moved a muscle.

He quickly swept up the glass and pulled her to her feet. She hissed out a breath and winced. Blood spurted from her hand, and like a careless Neanderthal, he snatched her up.

"I'm so sorry. I'm so sorry." He carried her into the bathroom and set her on the edge of the tub. "Stay here and hold your hand over the sink. I'll grab the first aid kit." He flipped on the faucet so the water flowed over her injured hand. "Don't move."

"Christian. I'm naked." She didn't meet his eyes, and her voice wavered.

He ran to the chest of drawers and pulled out a sweatshirt. "Lift your arms up for a minute."

She complied, and he carefully threaded her arms through the sleeves, afraid he'd exacerbate her wound. He placed her hand under the water again. Immediately, the sink was full of pink water.

Damn it. Cursing under his breath, he grabbed a towel and wrapped it tightly around her wrist. "Are you in a lot of pain? Are you okay? I'm so sorry." He couldn't ever be sorry enough. His pulse thundered in his temples while he gritted his teeth to maintain composure.

"I'm fine. It doesn't hurt, I swear. I think it's my finger, and those just bleed a lot." She gazed up from under her thick fringe of lashes. "Are you okay?"

"This is all my fault. I hurt you. We should go to the emergency room." Yes, the hospital. He'd take her to the hospital.

"I don't need the emergency room. Just need to stem the bleeding and a bandage or two." She looked back at her hand.

"Let me see." He forced himself back into commander mode and tamped down the feelings of panic threatening to consume him. He extended his exhales, working to slow down his shallow breathing and get a damn grip.

A few jagged slices marred her ring finger and the edge of her palm. She must've braced herself on the floor and cut herself on the glass.

"How did you get on the floor?" Shit, did he knock her out of bed?

"Well, you started flailing and yelling, which woke me up." She paused to lick her lips. "I got out of bed and was about to wake you up when your arm shot out and something on the nightstand went flying and shattered on the floor. I jumped out of the way, and clumsy me landed on my butt and put my hand down to catch my fall. My fault. I'm fine though, really." She nodded, as if trying to convince herself as well as him.

She sure as hell didn't look fine. Her golden skin was bone white, her pupils were dilated, and despite his sweatshirt reaching her knees, she was shaking. Shock, she was in shock.

"Don't try to make me feel better about this. I hurt you. This can't happen again." No way was he putting her in harm's way again, not from him.

"This?" Her eyes widened.

"This. Us. Together. Not happening again." He shook his head and bolted from the room.

He strode into his pantry to retrieve his first aid kit. He paused and leaned his forehead against the doorjamb and thumped his head a few times. Hard. He welcomed the shot of pain, of feeling. His stomach was jittery, and his hands shook.

This couldn't go on. Not just her, but his life like this.

A whine and small nudge against his leg alerted him to Olive on her hind legs, pawing at him.

"Not now." Damn pest.

She continued her efforts, and he cursed. He swooped down and picked her up, and she began licking his face and snuggling into his neck. He leaned back, and she covered his face with kisses. He closed his eyes for a moment, and the tension in his head eased. Okay, the dog was good at helping to bring him down from the brink.

But it didn't matter. It wasn't enough.

"Christian?" Her voice sounded stronger and he turned to see she'd entered the kitchen. He quickly put Olive down.

"Your little girl to the rescue?" She smiled and petted Olive, who'd trotted over to her.

"Not in time apparently. Come over to the counter." He took her hand and unwound the bloodstained towel. Without meeting her gaze, he cleaned it, applied antiseptic ointment, and wrapped gauze around the wounds. Once she was bandaged to his satisfaction, he retreated and replaced the first aid kit.

"Get dressed and I'll take you home." He shut the pantry door with finality.

"Home?"

Why did she sound surprised? Hurt? As if he'd allow her to stay here after what had happened?

"Yes, home." As if she'd want to stay.

"I'm fine, Christian. Why don't we watch a movie now?" Her voice was calm and measured.

His jaw dropped, and he swiveled his head to look at her. Her face was composed, and her cheeks were no longer colorless. What was wrong with her?

"No. I'm taking your home. Please don't argue with me on this." He tried to keep his voice civil. What the hell?

"I'm really fine. I'd rather stay." Her husky voice was resolute, and her rosy lips curved up.

"Look, I need to be alone. I don't need you hovering over me, and I don't need the guilt when this happens again. Because if I allow you to stay, it will. Now go get dressed. Please." He shoved down the spurt of regret at the hurt in her eyes.

She remained motionless, her golden eyes glistening with unshed tears.

Maybe he'd penetrated her stubborn resistance because she finally rose from the barstool and headed back to his bedroom. He gripped the counter, fighting for control. How much longer could he keep his shit together?

She returned a few minutes later, fully dressed, her expression as empty as his heart. She picked up her purse from the coffee table, walked to the front door, and pivoted toward him.

"I'm ready." Her jaw was set, and her spine rigid.

He grabbed his keys and marched to the door. He skirted around her, careful to avoid any contact. Something ugly swirled in his gut, and he'd be damned if he'd allow his demons to sully her again. No. Avoidance was the solution.

Quiet pervaded the ride to her cottage, and the only sound in the car was her soft measured breathing. She huddled against her car door, as far away from him as possible. Something twinged in his chest, but he quickly crushed it down. Maybe she was finally getting a damn clue.

If only he'd been man enough to stay away from her. Damn it. Now he'd caressed her soft skin, tasted her sweetness, and savored the sounds she made when she was aroused. Memories of tonight would torture him for the rest of his life. More fodder for his nightmares.

He cut the engine outside of the cottage, and she opened the door and stepped out. She paused and turned to him.

"Christian, please don't shut me out." Her tone turned urgent. "I'm really not hurt. I can help—"

"Goodbye, Kelly." Her words stabbed him. *Help.* He wasn't a goddamn dog she could save from the pound. Not a drug addict like her brother. No way would he be treated like another charity case.

"It's not goodbye." Her shoulders slumped; she shut the door and trudged to the cottage.

He waited until the light went on inside before he retreated down the driveway. His blood was ice in his veins, his brain blank, and his fingers talons around the steering wheel.

When he reached his house, he headed straight to the kitchen, where he poured two fingers of Glenfiddich from the bottle next to the refrigerator and slammed it in one shot. The sear of the whisky tore down his throat, but he welcomed the burning sensation. Better than the numbness. He closed his eyes and leaned his head back for a moment.

When would these fucking nightmares end? He'd been back from Iraq for two years now. He was no better than a fucking ten-year-old boy after watching horror flicks. Scared of monsters under the bed. An endless replay.

Guilt was a heavy cloak he couldn't seem to unfasten from his shoulders. Although logically he knew it wasn't all his fault, he couldn't shake the sense he wasn't good or capable enough to protect those close to him. Bad things happen in war, but he couldn't shake the guilt of more men dying when he was in part responsible for them. Something had to give. He'd hurt Kelly. His worst fear realized. Damn it.

He opened his eyes, grabbed a glass from the tall cabinet, and filled it with cool filtered water from the double-door refrigerator. He slugged the water down, much as he had the alcohol, and this time welcomed the soothing coolness down his parched throat. He set down the glass and leaned on the counter, gripping the edges until the pain registered.

Hell, he was only thirty-three years old. He'd begun to hope things would be different with Kelly.

After tonight, any glimmer of hope was extinguished.

Chapter 19

Kelly dropped her head onto her desk and squeezed her eyes closed, willing the exhaustion behind her gritty bloodshot eyes to dissipate. Keeping up a positive front for Kyle Warren took the last vestiges of her energy. Now that he'd left her office, she could no longer maintain her professional facade.

She'd managed to negotiate with his landlord for an extension of this month's rent and also set up an appointment with a pain-management doctor. They were working to wean Kyle off the heavy narcotics and to add in alternative therapies like acupuncture and over-the-counter options. His path wasn't easy, but the gratitude and hope in his eyes buoyed her up. She'd lent a helping hand. The rest was up to him.

If only helping herself was as natural as assisting others. Over a week had passed since she and Christian had finally taken one step forward and three steps back. Usually, work was the refuge she buried herself in, but the sleepless nights were killing her. The minute her head touched the pillow, their final evening together played like an interminable movie loop.

His caring response when she'd become upset about Peter at dinner offered her strength. The most incredible mind-blowing lovemaking session of her life—real or fantasy, mind you—gave her pleasure. Even his distress over believing he'd harmed her showed her how honorable he was. Once she dug beneath the outer package—and what a package, the handsome face, sexy muscular physique, and the Heathcliff silent and surly fantasy many women dreamed of—she'd fallen for the endearing, strong, real man.

Was she worse off now she knew they were not just perfectly matched in bed, but also potentially perfectly matched outside of it?

Her cell phone vibrated from her desk drawer.

"Kelly Prescott."

"Hi, Kelly. It's Melinda from Pups-4-Vets. How are you?"

"Busy. Nice to hear from you. What can I do for you?" Hopefully, some good news.

"Well, a couple things. I wanted to see if we could do a launch event to celebrate our partnership. Something down in Laguna at the center. Maybe bring a few dogs and their trainers to get the word out."

"What a great idea. I'd love it. We've got a big courtyard out in the back of the building, which would be perfect. Food, drinks, fun?" Perfect, a distraction.

"Exactly. And I wanted to run another idea by you. We love testimonials. Do you think Christian would be willing to share his story and how Olive is helping him? I spoke to him earlier this week, and he said she'd made a huge difference. I didn't ask, though, because I got the impression he's very private. Would you ask him?"

Crap. Kelly ran her tongue around her teeth. How to tell Melinda she and Christian weren't speaking?

"Well, I'm not sure he'd be willing to do it. I don't know if anybody besides you and me know about his PTS and, um, well, I haven't seen him in the last week or so. Maybe if you asked him. I don't think he'd be receptive to me right now." *Or answer the phone if I called.*

"Oh, I'd assumed you two... Did something happen?"

"Long story. If you ask him and he's in, I think it would be wonderful. If he refuses, we'll figure something out. I'm sure we can find another testimonial, right? Even if you pull in someone from outside Laguna?" Not ideal, but there was no way she could ask him.

"I'll call him again. I'm so excited you like the idea. I think it will be an excellent way to celebrate the new partnership."

"Great, let me know. I've got to run, but I'll look at some potential dates and get back to you." A spark of hope jumped in her belly—an excuse to see him on neutral ground. Would he agree to it?

"Thanks, Kelly. Talk to you soon."

"Knock, knock." Sophie poked her head in the doorway.

"Who's there?" She attempted a smile.

"Your favorite author and best friend in the world. I was running errands and wanted to check on you. Do you have time to grab some lunch?" Sophie leaned against the doorjamb, looking effortlessly cute in cropped denims and a navy-striped T-shirt.

"Sure, I've got time." Kelly grabbed her camel leather satchel, and they headed through the empty reception area and out the door.

Once they reached the quaint tree-lined street, Sophie asked, "Have you spoken with Christian?"

"Not a word." She shook her head and struggled

not to let her mood darken more. He'd remained true to his vow and not called, texted, or even sent a smoke signal.

"He and Nick hung out the other day. I guess he's starting to see a therapist?" Sophie shrugged.

"Well, wonderful. I hope it's helping." And she meant it. Christian was the most amazing man she'd ever met. His bravery and integrity were admirable.

"Let's head over to Laguna Coffee Company," Sophie said, and they turned onto S Coast Highway "Are you ready to talk about what happened?"

"It's private, and it sounds like he's working on it, but I just wish"—she swallowed down the hurt—"I wish he hadn't felt like he had to cut me off completely."

"I'm sorry, sweetie. I know this is really tough on you and you're really attracted to him, but it's probably for the best. You don't need another wounded bird." Sophie rubbed her shoulder.

"Stop calling him a wounded bird. He's not a damn wounded bird, and I'm not just attracted to him. I'm in love with him." Temper snapped through her voice.

"In love?" Sophie froze in her tracks, and her eyebrows flew up to her hairline. "*Love love*?"

"Yes, *love love*. I think he's the one. He's not a project. He's not Peter. He's not an addict. He went through hell and just needs more time to work through it. I think he can resolve his stuff and at least get to a point it's manageable. It doesn't make him less than." It made him real.

"No, no. I'm sorry, Kelly. You're right. I can't help but be protective of you, though. Well, if this is truly love and he reciprocates, let's hope he can come to you when he's ready. And if you're still waiting, then take it from there. I just don't want you to put your life on hold." Sophie's deep blue eyes were sincere.

"My life definitely isn't on hold. I've got a new house, live next door to my best friend, and my job is a perfect fit." She choked back a sob threatening to burst out. "I miss him." She *was* happy, but the taste of what life could be like if she and Christian were together haunted her.

Sophie wrapped her in a bear hug, and her shoulders softened. They resumed walking toward the restaurant.

"Melinda from Pups-4-Vets just called and wants to have a party at Peaceful Warrior. She's going to ask Christian to share his story about Olive."

"What a wonderful idea. Will he come? I can't quite picture Mr. Tall and Stoic giving a speech about his service dog, though."

"Not sure. But he had to be reserved to be a commander in the Special Forces. He couldn't have survived in the Middle East if he hadn't been tough, decisive, and courageous. And he fell for Olive like a little boy with his first puppy." She paused.

"Um, you weren't kidding about falling for him. He's always seemed kind and caring, just quiet with it. Day by day, right?" Sophie linked her arm through hers and smiled.

"You always make me feel better." The nervous restless energy she'd been plagued with since she'd left Christian softened.

"It's what friends are for. Okay, we're here and I'm starved. Let's order."

They joined the line to the counter.

Would he agree to speak at the party? Would they have the chance to reconnect? Could he recognize her compassion and caring didn't equate to pity, nor did those qualities make her codependent? If the man was too stubborn to see that she wasn't trying to rescue him, and she was simply trying to love him, he needed to figure it out. Before it was too late.

Chapter 20

Christian jiggled his leg and glared at his watch again. What the hell was it with doctor's offices and never staying on time for appointments? He'd been ten minutes early, and now he'd been in the sterile waiting room for almost forty minutes. He'd driven over to Santa Ana to see the private psychiatrist the VA had recommended. Screw it. He shoved out of the chair and strode to the door.

"Major Wolfe?"

A woman's voice called his name, and he turned back. Damn it.

She was short, plump, dressed in a navy sweater set and plaid skirt. Jesus, she looked like Angela Lansbury in *Murder, She Wrote*. This was the doctor they'd sent him to? How exactly did she relate to soldiers, because she sure as hell hadn't been out in the field?

Another dead end. His shoulders sagged. His morning was already shot, so he'd at least go in. Two well-worn wingback chairs dominated the powder-blue-wallpapered office. Shelves bursting with books lined the walls, and strands of sunlight filtered through the windows, warming the room. A tea tray with delicate china cups rested on a small wooden table between the chairs. He had traveled back in time to a 1960s' television show.

The plaid armchair was surprisingly comfortable,

and at least it wasn't a couch, or he'd feel like more of a loser than he already did. She perched on the seat opposite him, a yellow legal pad and pen in hand.

"May I call you Christian?" When he nodded, she continued, all business. "So I understand you've had some PTS symptoms, correct? Nightmares and anxiety?"

He cleared his throat. "Yeah, some memories from Iraq keep haunting me. Violent nightmares that won't stop."

"Tell me a little about your experiences there."

"Well, I led a ten-man A-Team and advised a hundred-man Iraqi Commando unit. We were close. They called me Captain Christian, thought it was funny my name was a religion." He rubbed the tight cords on the back of his neck. He felt more like Captain Loser now.

"Go on." She gestured with one hand and scribbled notes with the other.

"The Commando unit suffered a lot of losses while I was their senior adviser. Some were captured and tortured to death. I ran some rogue rescue mission attempts and lost a few of my men. One of my men lost an arm. It was my fault." He dropped his head and scrubbed his hands over his face.

"Why do you say so?"

"Look, I got reprimanded a few times—those missions were risky, not all approved." He surged to his feet and stalked to the window.

"Did you force your soldiers to participate?"

"No." He pivoted back to face her.

"It's been a few years, correct? Was there a specific episode that brought you into my office today?"

He nodded, returned to the chair, and sank into the cushions. "Yeah." Kelly's beautiful face popped into his mind.

When he failed to elaborate, she shifted gears. "We'll come back to it. What are you doing to work on the anxiety?"

"Working out used to be my medicine. I run, I box, I lift weights. Physical exhaustion helped me sleep with no dreams. Sometimes a drink will help." He shrugged. "I recently adopted a service dog, and she helps with the anxiety. I've also started meditating."

"Any improvement?" She scribbled a few notes on her notebook.

"I thought so, but not enough." He raked his fingers through his hair and massaged the back of his stiff neck. "It's just not enough."

"What made you realize it wasn't enough?"

"There's a woman I was becoming involved with and she..." Jesus, was he blushing? "She spent the night and I had a nightmare and she got hurt."

"Oh dear. Is she okay?" She sipped her tea and peered at him through her thick glasses.

"Well, her hand was cut, and I cleaned it up and took her home. I'm assuming she's fine by now." He hoped.

"You haven't spoken to her since then? You don't know how she is?" Her eyebrows arched over her spectacles. So much for the nonjudgmental therapist.

"It's better this way. She's better off." He ignored the tightening in his chest.

"Did she say so?" Her calm tone grated like the incessant whirr of a buzz saw.

"Well, no, she said she was fine. She didn't want to go home." And the hurt look in her eyes haunted him.

"But you took her anyway?" Angela Lansbury jotted another note on her pad.

"She was bleeding." He shot to his feet, gritted his teeth to keep his voice level. "What else was I supposed to do? I hurt her, and I care about her too much to keep her in harm's way."

"So you're deciding what's best for her? Is she a passive sort, then? Weak?" She quirked a brow.

"Passive? No, she's incredibly brave and clever and compassionate. She's the most amazing woman I've ever met in my life and deserves a real man." The words tumbled out.

"Hmmmm…" She scribbled more notes.

"Look, I don't want to talk about Kelly. This is about me." He closed his eyes and worked to shut out the vision of her face.

"Are you in love with her?"

He whirled back to face her, his jaw slack. "Huh?"

"Love. Are you in love with Kelly?" Her tone remained calm.

"Look, Doctor, I didn't come here to talk about Kelly. I came to see if you could do anything to help me. I need help."

"Please sit down, Christian." She paused while he sank into the chair again. "You probably don't want to hear this, but your issues aren't uncommon. You can get better, but there's a chance you'll have nightmares and events trigger you for the rest of your life. I'm not saying it's the case, but it's a possibility. It's also possible you can beat this."

"So there is a chance I can be free from this?" He

gripped the arms on the chair.

"Your willingness to work on it gives you a chance. You can also acquire more coping techniques. Be patient. Eliminate the things that set you off. Also, I think if we met once a week and dug into what happened in Iraq and Afghanistan, it would help you to express it all out loud to let them go."

"Every week?" Great, from major to a sensitive dude going to weekly therapy. Could he feel any more emasculated? Weak?

"It doesn't make you weak." Could she read his mind?

"Well, I'm really busy and..." Was he making up excuses?

"Look, Major Wolfe. You sought me out because you said you were ready to try to beat this. If you want to give up and accept your current situation, nobody would blame you. If you want to fight and see if you can improve it, then weekly therapy is one avenue I suggest."

"Fine." Challenging a military man to fight was like waving a red flag in front of the proverbial bull. Irresistible.

"Does next Tuesday at ten work for you?" She'd pulled out an old-fashioned day planner covered in some type of flower pattern.

"Fine." He crossed his arms and dug his fingers into his triceps.

He returned to the parking lot, but he wasn't willing to drive home just yet. A carved wooden bench underneath an enormous palm tree beckoned to him. He sat and closed his eyes, inhaled a deep breath. Would it really solve anything if he shared some of the hideous things that had happened overseas? Could he stop the panic attacks and nightmares? If so, would he be the type of man Kelly deserved? One who could commit to her?

His eyes popped open. Love? He jolted at the trilling of his phone. Was it Kelly?

He recognized the Pups-4-Vets number. Melinda was fretting over Olive like a mother who'd just sent her child away to kindergarten. She'd called numerous times already.

"Olive is still fine." He didn't bother with a greeting.

"Hi, Christian. I'm sure she is, and it's part of why I'm calling. I've got a little favor to ask that will help our other dogs find their special human."

Uh-oh. "Yes?"

"I'm sure Kelly told you we've decided to have a party at Peaceful Warrior to celebrate our partnership and promote the program. It could make a huge difference for those vets in need."

"Okay." As he and Kelly weren't speaking these days, she definitely hadn't told him.

"Well, of course, we'll want you and Olive to attend."

"Sure." Shit. His temples began to throb.

"What would really help is if you would be willing to share a brief testimonial about what a difference Olive is making and how glad you are to be part of the program." Melinda rushed the words out.

Was she kidding? The pounding in his head increased its staccato tempo. "I don't—" Hell no. Tell the world he had PTS? He'd worked hard the last two years to transition to a regular civilian life, to put the past behind him. He snorted. As if that plan was going well.

"Kelly told me you're very private and I respect your privacy, but if you feel any kind of duty to other returning soldiers, your transparency would be huge. Before you decline, think how much this could not only help others but could help you too."

Duty. He gritted his teeth. He'd screwed up in Iraq. Lost men. Davidson, who'd lost his arm, still haunted him. If he'd moved a little quicker, reacted a little sooner, he could have saved him. Saved all of them.

"Christian." Melinda's even voice yanked him back to the present.

"What would I have to do?" Damn it.

"Don't feel like you have to share too many personal details. Just share what you've dealt with, maybe give an example, and explain how Olive has helped you and how the dogs can make an enormous difference."

Damn it. "Okay. Okay, I'll do it." He expelled a breath. "When?"

"I'm coordinating with Kelly. Either she or I will be in touch. Thank you so much, Christian."

After they hung up, he closed his eyes again. Kelly's beautiful face filled his vision. He couldn't stop remembering the feel of her silky skin, her distinctive sweet cinnamon scent, her bright golden eyes, and clever, warm personality. He'd never experienced the emotions she evoked in him. He could picture a future with her as his partner, his lover, and his best friend. Damn, he missed the laughter, the chemistry, the compassion, and sweetness she radiated. But he refused to subject her to a repeat performance of his nightmares. Refused to drag her down with his PTS. Refused to be a burden.

Maybe helping others would make a difference. Olive was a step in the right direction, and he would return to meditation and see Angela Lansbury every week. He'd do it for himself and for the potential of Kelly.

Duty—he had a duty to be a better man, and until when, and if, that happened, he'd be a single one.

Chapter 21

Kelly's cell phone rang, and she grabbed it and checked the screen. Was Christian finally calling? Her shoulders tensed when she saw her father's name. Her nerves couldn't survive a confrontation right now. Why would he call her unless it was an emergency? She jolted upright in her office chair.

"Dad? Is everything okay? Did something happen to Mom?"

"Hello, Kelly. No, your mother is fine. It's business. I need to speak with you about Hexaun." His voice sounded strained.

"Hexaun? Are you finally going to remove yourself as counsel?" Thank goodness. Those corrupt crooks didn't deserve representation as stellar as her father's.

"I need to talk to you in person, not over the phone. Is there any way you can come down? Or if not, I'll drive up to Laguna."

"Drive up to Laguna? Now?" Would her father actually come to her? Circumstances must be dire.

"It's urgent."

"I'll come down there. To the office?" Today hadn't been a model of productivity at Peaceful Warrior, and she could always catch up after hours. She'd never heard her father's voice like this.

"Yes, but before you leave, you need to check today's issue of Reuters and read the article on

Hexaun."

"Okay. I'll be there in the next hour or two." Holy crap, what was going on?

She accessed Reuters online and right there on the front page, three names she'd never wanted to see associated together screamed at her: Hexaun, the Prescott Law Firm, and the Department of Justice. What was going on?

She opened the article and a pit formed in her belly. Oh no, it couldn't be. The DOJ was apparently launching an investigation into the anxiety drug, Dixastra, the one she'd told her father about. A whistleblower from inside the company claimed Dixastra had been found to cause a rare cancer and employees of Hexaun had willfully covered it up. The article named Prescott Law Firm as counsel of record for Hexaun. Her mouth dropped open to see a quote from her father stating Hexaun would be cleared of any wrongdoing. Crap, crap, crap.

She tossed her phone into her briefcase and raced to her car. If her father didn't separate himself from Hexaun, they could topple his entire empire. The firm would be ruined. He could be disbarred, or worse, if it were shown he had any knowledge. Even though she didn't want the legacy for herself, her father had dedicated his life—at the price of his family—to building the firm. In the law, reputation was everything. What if her father ended up personally liable? Not common, but depending upon what the DOJ might be able to show, if her dad knew the client was committing fraud, his attorney-client privilege went out the window.

She huffed out a breath. Think. Think. What now?

When she got in her car, she activated her Bluetooth and called her contact Jason Myers from Hexaun.

He answered on the first ring. "Kelly, hi. I figured you might call."

"Jason, what's going on? Was it you? How did all of this happen?"

"You don't work at Prescott anymore, Kelly, so you'll be fine." His voice betrayed no emotion at all.

Her head began to pound. "Yes, but my father—"

"Look, you know how these things work. It's gotten too big. Too many people involved. I had to go to the DOJ. Another study was born and buried by Hexaun, and it's even worse than the first one. This drug will kill people. With a rare form of cancer there's no treatment for. It was time to bring it to light. I can't continue working for someone like this."

"Do they know it was you?" The pharmaceutical industry was powerful and could tear an individual apart.

"I'm sure they suspect. But I can't be silent anymore. I've resisted doing the reports, but it's out of control here. No amount of money is worth peoples' lives."

"This is terrible. My father called me, and I'm on my way to his office right now. I'm going to see if he'll withdraw now it's at this level." Although the likelihood was slim, she had to attempt to help.

"Didn't he boot you out of there? Rumor was he disowned you?"

"So much for privacy. Where'd you hear that?" Lovely. How had it gotten out? Probably Robert, the jerk. He was also tied to this, complicit in the knowledge. Maybe he had whitewashed it all, and her father was unaware of how far the corruption went? Maybe he believed the whistleblower was simply a disgruntled employee looking for revenge? She gripped the steering wheel, visualizing it as Robert's scrawny neck, and squeezed tight.

Silence.

"It doesn't matter. I've got to try. Prescott is my name too, even if I'm no longer there." Besides not wanting her father to lose his firm or worse, go to jail, she had to try to help.

"I hear you're at a veterans' nonprofit." Jason changed the subject.

"I am. I love it. It's so much different, but so much more rewarding." And thank goodness she'd left before the shit hit the fan with Hexaun.

"And so much more you. They're lucky to have you as their avenging angel. Good for you. Besides all of this, everything else okay?" She and Jason were friends.

Christian's dark face flashed before her eyes. *Okay* wasn't the word she'd choose. Heartbroken, lonely, or devastated were more apt descriptions. But she would survive. She always did.

"All good. Thanks. I'm going to focus on the road. Let's stay in touch."

Her mind raced back to the day she'd been reviewing the clinical data. She'd been shocked to discover the studies revealed a statistically significant association between use of the drug and the development of cancer. Because the specific type of cancer was so rare, it could only be the drug causing it. At the point she'd been researching, Hexaun had just applied for a supplemental usage of the drug, and the FDA denied it. The FDA denial would cost the company millions in lost revenue.

Concerned with the scenario, she'd dug deeper and discovered a newly published clinical study in one of the most distinguished national medical journals. She'd been horrified to discover a few of the authors had been paid by the Hexaun Company to write the article and publish biased information, which basically amounted to fraud. And in her eyes, murder.

Luckily, she didn't encounter any traffic as she flew down the 5 to downtown San Diego. She pulled into the law firm parking garage and swallowed the nerves tickling her throat. Her father had sought her out, and she'd tell him what she knew. She couldn't control what Alistair Prescott III did with the information, but she'd divulge her discoveries.

Her heels clicked on the marble lobby floor as she entered the building. The security guard, bless his heart, showed no sign of surprise when she approached his desk, and simply nodded his head and clicked the security access for the elevators for her. At least someone still had some loyalty to her. Most people had been shocked at her exit, but her phone hadn't burned up with calls or texts checking on her welfare.

She practiced the deep breathing she and Sophie had learned in yoga. Her heart raced, her palms sweated, and the pit in her belly showed no signs of dissipating. *Keep it together, girl.* She strode down the hallway directly to her father's lavish corner office. Surprised faces peeped up from the secretaries' cubicles she passed, like groundhogs checking for spring. It hadn't been long since she'd been banished from her father's domain. She knocked perfunctorily before entering.

"You came." He didn't budge from his throne.

She gasped at his gaunt appearance and the deep grooves bracketing his mouth and eyes. Although she'd left only weeks ago, he'd aged years.

"Yes." She paused, then sat down and folded her hands in her lap. Gripped her fingers tight.

"I've got to talk to you about Hexaun and this investigation. I keep thinking of what you were trying to tell me before you left. I've got questions."

She nodded. "Okay, let me tell you the facts I uncovered."

She poured out the details, the call from Jason, and the insider worry at the company because the tampering was escalating. More careless. More criminal.

He sat up straighter in his chair as she continued, and his expression hardened. He held up a hand. "Hold on a damn minute. Are you telling me several people in the company know about it? There were really thousands of buried reports? Deleted emails?" His eyes were obsidian chips, a sure sign his temper was about to blow.

"Yes, it's what I was trying to tell you when I quit. I couldn't be a part of it. Dad, innocent people could die, and they don't care. No client is worth this. Please recuse yourself. Please step away." She lifted her eyes to him and allowed the full force of her emotion to show. Damn it, despite it all, he was her father and she loved him. They'd never been close and most likely never would, but she didn't want to see him ruined.

He picked up the phone, punched in a number, and barked out, "Get in here. Now." He slammed the phone back down.

She twisted her hands together. Who had he called?

The door opened, and Robert entered. *Aha.* It was all starting to make sense. Robert. How nice to have the anger directed at him and not her for once.

Robert's eyes narrowed when he saw her, but to his credit, he didn't flinch. How had she not seen how cold he was? How calculating? Had she been so wrapped up in her work and avoiding true emotional entanglements she'd missed it altogether?

"Alistair. Kelly." He nodded to each of them and approached the desk.

"Sit." Her father in a temper was a sight to behold.

Robert sat.

"What the hell is going on with Hexaun? Why the hell didn't you tell me they'd deleted all these adverse event reports? That they'd paid off experts to write the article? What the hell is wrong with you?" He slapped his hand on his massive desk, his expression thunderous.

"I did tell you. What's this about?" He shrugged and delivered the smooth lie as he looked between Kelly and her father.

"You told me there were a few minor reports buried, nothing major. You neglected to inform me of the rare cancer and the high probability of it infecting people taking the drug. You also neglected to discern between criminal fraud and questionable business practices. Don't you know the difference?"

"Oh, Kelly's exaggerating, like she always has. Come on, Alistair. It's really not as bad as it sounds." His expression was smug.

She'd love to smack it off his face.

"No, Robert, Kelly isn't exaggerating. If you had an ounce of integrity, the kind of ethics that are the backbone of this law firm, you would have given me the full picture. I trusted you to keep me apprised, and you purposefully withheld information. Now your carelessness could destroy my firm." He rose and glared down at Robert.

She should really consider getting a raised platform for her desk. The dais did create a great way to exude power. Although the situation was serious, she couldn't help but enjoy Robert's dressing down.

"Now go get me all of those reports, not just the redacted bullshit you gave me before. I'm going through them personally. And if you want to have any chance at keeping your Bar license, you'll do it. Now." He barked the orders at Robert, who leapt to his feet and scurried out of the room.

He sank back into his seat and shifted his gaze to her. "I owe you an apology."

It was a good thing she was sitting down, because if she'd been standing, she would have fallen over. She opened and closed her mouth a few times, but no sound emerged. Her father had never apologized to anyone over anything. Ever. She sat there like a dolt and stared at him.

He laughed self-deprecatingly and rubbed his forehead. She'd never seen him exhibit any hint of vulnerability before.

"I treated you unfairly when you resigned. I was so angry. So disappointed—" His continued to stare at his desk.

"Dad—"

"Let me finish. It needs saying. I wanted you to

take over the firm. You're a terrific attorney. Brilliant. You've made me incredibly proud. You had the guts to stand up to me when nobody ever has. Nobody. So I owe you an apology." His gaze lifted, and his eyes weren't the customary chilly onyx. No, they were almost warm.

Proud of her? Brilliant? Had she stepped through the looking glass and landed in a parallel universe?

"I've rendered you speechless—never thought I'd see the day." A rueful smile curved his lips. "Look, you've made your choices and I understand. I'll take care of this situation. I won't allow this firm to be destroyed. Thank you for coming today, especially after how I treated you."

"Thank you. Thanks for listening. Although this isn't the place for me, I don't want you to lose it either."

They sat in awkward silence. They'd never been close. Never been soft. After thirty years, their relationship wasn't bound to suddenly change. But his apology and his compliments went a long way to soothing the little girl inside her who'd just wanted her daddy to love her.

"Any chance you'd reconsider—"

"Not a chance in hell." She cut him off with a vigorous shake of her head.

They laughed. Awkward silence again.

"Well, I better get going back up to Laguna." She rose from her chair.

"Wait. Kelly. I'm sorry about all the disowning business. I never meant to go through with it. Your mother was furious—"

"Right, so furious she didn't even call me

181

afterward?" It still rankled. Again, her mom had always been distant, but those expectations and a child's desire for love and approval apparently never died.

"We've never been the model parents, and when Peter started having problems, we just...we didn't handle it well. I know you ended up bearing the brunt of his addiction and his attempts to detox." He stepped down from his throne and approached her. "Please don't doubt we both love you and you are welcome here or at home anytime."

His eyes again revealed a vulnerability she'd never seen. Maybe he was getting softer with old age? He pulled her into a self-conscious hug and patted her back a few times.

"Thanks, Dad. I love you too. Please take care of this. And I know I'm personally biased, but feel free to fire Robert. He's an ass."

"Yes, he is. I'll get to the bottom of all of this." He frowned. "You're okay in Laguna? The job? Money?"

"I love it. The salary is crappy, but I don't care." She smiled at him as she backed toward the door.

"Bye, Kelly." His tone was gentle.

"Bye." She closed the door behind her and walked back to the bank of elevators. With each step toward the exit, her shoulders relaxed and the pit in her belly softened.

Perhaps she and her father would one day move past everything that had happened. They'd never be a sitcom family or realistically they'd never be close, but her heart settled a tiny bit. Maybe they would never have a close, warm loving bond some people were lucky enough to enjoy, but he'd apologized and made an effort.

On the drive back to Laguna, her mind flashed to one of the last times she'd seen Peter. Lounging on the couch trying to detox on his own, shaking, shivering, sweating, and begging to die. Her brother's demons ultimately took him. Perhaps it was time she forgave herself for not being able to save him. Life was a series of choices, and each person ultimately was in the driver's seat of their destiny.

Christian obviously had his own issues, although she could see the positive path he was pursuing with Olive, meditation, and therapy. He was imperfect, but wasn't she too? Her heart refused to accept that Christian wasn't her soul mate. Her gut instinct urged her to find a way to reconcile with him, but her logical brain cautioned her to protect herself.

She parked in front of Peaceful Warrior and stared up at the building where she'd begun her new life, the life true to her values and ethics. If she could transform her professional life to align with her dreams, why couldn't she transform her personal life to fulfill her deepest desires?

Chapter 22

Christian parked his Jeep, tucked Olive under his arm, and marched into Peaceful Warrior. His eyes burned because he hadn't slept a wink last night. He wasn't exactly the poster child for disabled veterans and service dogs. He'd been responsible for some of his soldiers not returning home, he'd resigned his commission early, and he still carried a hefty duffle bag of issues. How the hell had he ended up agreeing to not only attend the event but to also give a speech?

The hallway leading to the courtyard was deserted. His heartrate accelerated with each step closer to the doorway, but he swallowed the panic rising in his throat and kept Olive snuggled close. Damn, he loved the little creature.

When he reached the open back door, he did a double take. The pleasant yet usually generic outdoor courtyard area resembled an Independence Day parade. Red, white, and blue streamers were woven through the trees and rustled in the ocean breeze. Clusters of balloons floated from picnic tables covered with bright platters of food.

Melinda waved to him and approached with an enormous yellow dog sporting a patriotic stars-and-stripes bandana.

Olive pawed his arm, eager to interact with the animal five times her size. She yipped and wiggled until he set her down, and then she hopped around on her stumpy legs.

Melinda laughed. "They were buddies at the facility. Brody was heartbroken when Olive threw him over for you."

He grinned, the dogs' playful interaction a shot of serotonin to his system, instantly relaxing him. Their cavorting was a visceral reminder of how much the dogs' simple presence could help people. Add in specialized training and job tasks, and the animals were invaluable additions to any veteran's life. He could do this.

He crouched down and rubbed Brody's belly, and Olive sidled in. "So how many dogs are here today?" He kept his attention on the animals, studiously avoiding scanning the courtyard for Kelly.

"We brought a dozen, with all different skill sets. Kelly sent invitations to all the vets on Peaceful Warrior's list, and we used our database too. We should have a few other successful adopters attending with their dogs as well."

"Oh? So somebody else could give the speech?" Maybe he could just hang out and show off Olive?

"No, Christian. You are the perfect person to do this. You're a leader, someone people respect. It will mean so much coming from you." Melinda smiled again.

He closed his eyes for a moment. Damn it. He needed to get over himself. A familiar cinnamon scent assaulted his nostrils.

When his eyes flew open, a familiar pair of golden legs sporting strappy red sandals was within reach. He automatically lifted his hand from Brody's belly, wanting to stroke the silky skin. He jerked it back. What the hell was wrong with him?

"You made it." He shifted his gaze up, struggling not to stare at the breezy little white sundress Kelly wore. Although, *damn, she was gorgeous.*

"Yeah." He stood.

"Good. You look good." Her voice was huskier than usual, but he couldn't see her caramel eyes behind her enormous sunglasses.

"You too." Mouthwatering was more appropriate.

"So how have you—"

"How are you?"

"You first." Could he spit out a full sentence? That boded well for his time at the podium. Not.

"I'm fine. Busy. Glad this event is finally here." She leaned down and scratched Brody's head.

"Yeah." And that was the best he had.

"Well, I need to make sure everything's all set. I'll let you know when we're going to start the program." Kelly spun and hurried off, her skirt fluttering around those toned golden legs.

"I'm going to introduce Brody around. Grab a drink and check out all the information stations." Melinda didn't comment on the extremely awkward scene she'd just been forced to witness, and he appreciated it.

People and dogs streamed into the courtyard, and the noise level rose, punctuated with laughter, happy barks, and chatter. Nick, Sophie, Brandt, and Alyssa entered with Bailey strolling sedately beside them. How in the world had they managed to get the excitable mutt to relax? He waved, and they joined him and Olive on the sidelines of the rapidly growing party.

"Great turnout. You ready for this?" Nick asked as he bent down and scratched Olive's head.

"Yeah, it's not a big deal." So why were his palms sweaty?

"Christian, it *is* a big deal." Sophie rubbed his shoulder. "Your story will resonate with so many people, and it'll help them and the organization. I think it's wonderful you're doing this."

"I hope so. There sure are a lot of people here." And he would not allow it to deter him from doing this right.

"So where's Kelly?" Alyssa asked, searching through the crowd.

He shrugged. Nobody expected him to know the answer to that question, right? He'd only seen her for the first time today in almost a month. Damn it, she should be by his side.

"Is that a doggie kissing booth?" Sophie pointed to a stand set up with a hand-painted sign proclaiming Kissing Booth $1. "Do you think they'd let Bailey work it?"

"Ooooh, she'd love it. We'll see you guys in a little while." Alyssa and Sophie headed toward the booth with Bailey galloping behind.

"So, man, you okay with this?" Brandt asked.

"Yeah, just ready to get it over with." Apparently, his earlier reply wasn't too convincing. Olive pawed his shin, and he swooped her up into the crook of his arm.

"You'll be great." Nick said.

"Major." A quiet voice spoke from behind him.

Private Roger Davidson. He hadn't heard his private's voice since they'd returned over two years ago. He slowly pivoted to face Davidson and braced himself for the assault. Davidson saluted him with his artificial limb. He stood tall, his hair neat and still military short. A cute brunette cradling a baby flanked his side. She smiled at Christian.

He saluted back. Habit. "Davidson, good to see you."

"That's gotta be the ugliest dog I've ever seen. You sure they didn't cheat you with that thing? Maybe give you a rat?" The young man's familiar grin split his wide face.

He'd never thought to see Davidson smile at him again. Roger had been the smart aleck of the team, always cracking jokes and making everyone laugh with his brand of snarky humor. After the last mission, when his arm had blown off, he certainly hadn't grinned at Christian and he definitely hadn't cracked any jokes.

Recovering his wits, he managed to reply. "Don't you insult my Olive. When she works that kissing booth, she'll rake in the bucks. She's a beauty."

They all laughed. Brandt and Nick backed away with a casual wave, leaving him alone with his former soldier.

"This is my wife Denise and our son Bobby."

Denise shook his hand, and the baby gurgled.

"You've got a beautiful family." That had to be good, right? Wasn't Denise the girlfriend who'd been waiting on him at home?

"Yes, I'm lucky." Davidson nodded and looked at his little family with pride. "Could I speak to you, sir? Privately?"

"Of course." Christian's gut clenched. Shit. "We can go inside."

They left the courtyard, and Christian led Davidson

to the meditation room. They shut the door and sat down on a couple of the hard-back chairs. Olive leapt into his lap, circled twice, and plopped down for a nap.

Davidson's posture was ramrod straight, and he looked Christian dead in the eye. "Sir, may I speak freely?"

"I'm not your commanding officer anymore. You can speak to me however you like."

"Okay." He gave a short, sharp nod. "I want to apologize."

"Apologize?" Christian relaxed his jaw. What the hell?

"Yes, sir. I should have been in touch with you a long time ago and let you know everything was okay. We left things on poor terms after I was hurt. You aren't responsible."

"Damn well I was responsible. I gave you a direct order, you followed it, and look what happened." He pushed out of the chair and stalked around the room, with Olive cradled under his arm.

"No, sir. My job, my role, and what I signed up for was to follow orders. You did your job. I did mine. It's war. It's nobody's fault, except maybe the person who hit me. But then again, they were only doing their job too."

"But—" He halted, unwilling to turn and face his man yet.

"Sir, if I may. Let me finish. I was devastated. Who wouldn't be? It hurt like hell. I had to learn how to do things like putting on my shoes and zipping my fly all over again. I'm not going to lie—I miss my damn arm. But Denise loves me anyway. She didn't care. We've got a kid now. A lifetime in front of us. Hell, it's a scar.

But that's what I signed up for. I've never blamed you, and I hate to see you might be thinking I did. You aren't God, and you aren't responsible for everything."

"I know I'm not God." Did he? "If I'd been faster, I could have pulled you out of the way in time. I just—" He turned back to Davidson.

"Sir, again. No disrespect, but you can take me off your list of people or things to be guilty for. I have an amazing life. I'm proud I served my country. Do I wish I had two arms? Hell, yeah. But I don't. Life goes on." He shrugged.

Christian was speechless. He'd obsessed hours over this man and how miserable he must be. What a selfish idiot he was. Life moved on, and obviously Davidson was light years ahead of him in that regard.

"You sure?" He didn't know what else to say. Had he really been torturing himself for years over something that wasn't real? Could he let it go?

"Yes, sir. I just am sorry I didn't check in with you sooner." Davidson certainly looked happy.

"Well, thank you. I'm glad to hear it."

"You don't seem convinced, but I'll prove it to you by paying to kiss the ugliest beast I've ever seen." Davidson reached out and scratched Olive's grizzled head.

"Deal." He shook his former soldier's new hand. They returned to the sunlight together and stopped at the vision before him.

Chapter 23

Kelly stood silhouetted in the doorway, motes of dust floating in the sunshine framing her. "There you are. Okay, I'm going to start the program in ten minutes. Could you come over to the stage in the next few?" She was all business.

His chest tightened. She was so damn stunning. As usual, he was struck speechless.

"Hi, ma'am. Roger Davidson." He reached out and shook Kelly's hand. "Just needed to talk to my former commander. Looking forward to learning more about the organization."

"Hi, Roger. Pleased to meet you. You were overseas with Major Wolfe?" Her brows rose, and she flicked her gaze between the two of them.

"Yes, ma'am. He saved my life. I was just thanking him."

"That's wonderful. Well, I'll see you both outside. Three minutes please." Kelly flashed her pearly whites at Davidson, turned on her stiletto heels, and sauntered away.

"Wow. I mean, don't get me wrong, I love my Denise, but wow." Davidson's jaw hung open.

"Stop drooling. That's an order. She's the general counsel, the one who set up this whole program. The one who found me Olive." The one who made him crave a different future.

"I'm not drooling, sir. Just appreciation. Is she single?" Davidson slanted a sly gaze at him.

"No. I mean, yes." Damn it. Regardless, he'd blown his chance. Even so, the possessive urge to claim her pulsed inside him.

"Look, I'm going to hit the bathroom. Be right out." He entered the bathroom, set Olive down, and approached the sink. He turned on the cold water and splashed his face, soothed his overheated skin. Davidson didn't blame him. Didn't hate him. He had moved on and created a real life with a wife and child. A family.

"Olive, did I screw up?"

Olive barked, and her head lolled to the side, her pink tongue hanging out of her mouth, pondering her reply.

"I'm an idiot. I sabotaged a chance with the only woman who's ever seemed to accept me. Chased her off, and all the while, Davidson didn't blame me at all. Is it too late?"

Olive tilted her head the other way, still undecided. She yipped and scratched his shin, so he swooped down and cradled her close again. Her bug eyes peered into his face, and she nodded. Was she agreeing with him? Had he lost it?

"Man, the presentation is starting. You in here?" Nick called from the doorway.

"Yeah, yeah. I'm coming." He squared his shoulders and shifted back to his military mindset. No time for fear. Time to risk it all.

He followed his friend over to the side of the stage, and Nick, Sophie, Brandt, and Alyssa clustered around him, offering silent support. A strong breeze blew across his skin, and Olive licked his chin.

"Welcome, everyone. Can I have your attention please?" Kelly called over the microphone. The crowd quieted. "Please gather around for our brief program. I promise the dog-kissing booth will reopen in a few minutes." Laughter danced across the courtyard.

Mr. Williams, Susan, and Melinda from Pups-4-Vets flanked Kelly on the wooden stage.

"First, thanks so much for coming today. I'm Kelly Prescott, and for those of you I haven't met yet, hello. I'm thrilled to introduce our newest partnership and a program you'll love. As you may have noticed, we've got dogs everywhere. Not just fun, wonderful pets but highly accomplished animals trained to make life easier for people, whether it's purely physical assistance, like opening doors and guiding wheelchairs, or emotional support. These dogs have all been saved from a shelter, a rescue group, or off the street. Pups-4-Vets tests their temperament, and if they are a fit, they go into a year of specialized training. It's an amazing program all the way around." People hooted and cheered. Christian's shoulders relaxed as the applause filled the courtyard.

"Wait, the best part is it's free. Generous donors and grants fund Pups-4-Vets. Melinda will be available all afternoon to answer questions. But we thought it would be powerful for you to hear about a success story and meet the first Pups-4-Vets Dog/Peaceful Warrior collaboration. I'm happy to introduce Major Christian Wolfe and his partner, Olive."

Christian expelled the breath he hadn't realized he'd been holding. Well, here went nothing. He climbed the three steps to the stage. Suddenly, the sun seemed too vivid, the noise too loud, the sea of faces a blur. Thank God he had his sunglasses on.

Damn it. He wouldn't lose his shit here, in front of a crowd. He was a soldier who'd been rewarded for discipline and bravery. He gazed down at Olive and her ridiculous alien face. She barked twice, "Get going."

"Hi. My name is Christian Wolfe, and this is Olive. I don't know if I'm a success story per se, but I can say this little dog has made a huge difference in my life over the last month. When I met her, I didn't know animals were trained to help with emotional and mental side effects from war. I assumed a service dog was a big brawny Lab or German shepherd who would help people missing a limb or in a wheelchair. Help with those external wounds, the ones everyone can see." He paused. Swallowed.

You could hear a pin drop.

"Most people looking at me can't tell I'm wounded. I thought I'd be in the military for life. I resigned my commission early, after four tours, because I've got PTS.

"How does it work? Well, I have panic attacks. Anxiety attacks. Nightmares that would make hanging out on Elm Street look more like *Sesame Street*. I'm not the same man I was a decade ago. I may never be the same man who joined ROTC during my stint at San Diego State University. But life goes on, right?" He paused, his throat parched.

A slender golden hand offered him a bottle of ice water, and he chugged half of it. Kelly smiled and nodded, encouraging him to finish, and remained by his side.

"Except I wasn't really moving on. I was lying to myself that everything was okay. But it's not. I'm working to get a handle on the guilt, the memories staining my consciousness, the men I lost overseas. Hell, I'm even going to a therapist now. But this dog, Olive." Her ears perked up at her name, and she wiggled her little butt in excitement. "This dog helps my blood pressure go down and my headaches dissipate. All I know is I'm coping, she's helping me, and now I have hope that one day, I'll feel at least a new normal. And hope is a big deal when you've come from a place where it doesn't exist."

Clapping and cheers escalated until the courtyard filled with it. He smiled, realizing he'd meant every word he'd said. So much for trying to write a speech or note cards. People responded to his speech like his soldiers used to respond to his orders.

Kelly touched his arm, and he turned. He couldn't see her eyes, but her face was soft, and she smiled warmly. Compassion emanated from her, not pity. Had it been that way all along?

"Thanks so much, Christian. Okay, everyone, Melinda, Mr. Williams, and I are available for questions, and we've got plenty of food, dogs to pet, and we encourage you to hang out and socialize. Now Melinda will take Olive over to the kissing booth, because who wouldn't to kiss that face?" Kelly joked as she took over again.

"Wait. I've got one more thing to say." Christian stopped her. Grasped her hand. She jolted and looked down at where his tanned fingers covered hers. He pulled her to his side and held her close. She stiffened.

The crowd clapped and cheered, and someone hooted in approval.

"Today's a day of confessions. As a military

leader, I prided myself on being brave and following my instincts. Unfortunately, since I met Kelly Prescott, I've been a coward and an idiot."

The crowd quieted again, and Kelly's gaze burned into him.

"This woman is the most incredible woman I've ever met. She's an accomplished attorney, a brilliant mind, a compassionate heart, and the most beautiful woman I've ever seen. She's special. One of a kind."

Kelly's hand had gone limp in his, and he risked a sideways glance. Her rosy lips were parted in surprise.

"I was afraid since I have PTS, I wasn't worthy of her. I ran. I was a coward. I didn't fight for her because I didn't believe I deserved her. I mean, look at her. Today I had a conversation with a soldier I respect that set my head on straight. He reminded me life is short, and I'm not going to waste another minute."

The crowd whooped again, Roger Davidson's voice clear over the noise, and Kelly's cheeks flushed pink.

"Kelly, I'm asking you up here, in front of all these people, to give me another chance." His breath stuck in his throat as he waited for her reply.

"No pressure," Brandt shouted. Laughter peppered through the crowd.

He turned away from the microphone, shoved his sunglasses up onto his head so she could see his eyes. He gently removed hers and clasped both of her hands in his. Tears sparkled in her golden eyes, and she bit her lip as she stared. He allowed everything he was feeling to show in his gaze and prayed it was enough.

"Yes." She laughed and threw her arms around his neck. He picked her up and swung her around while

Olive yapped at their ankles. They left the stage together.

"Bravo, man." Nick lightly punched his shoulder and grinned. "Can I buy you two a celebratory beer?"

"Pretty sure they're free, but you've always been cheap." Everyone laughed.

"Let me take Olive over to the kissing booth." Melinda plucked Olive up and carted her over to the other side of the crowd.

Nick pulled two longneck beers out of a bucket of ice, untwisted the tops, and handed it to each of them. "There you go. Don't say I never bought you a present."

They clinked the bottles in a toast.

"So does this mean you two are an item?" Alyssa asked with a sly smile.

"Those googly eyes gave them away from the start." Sophie joined in the teasing with a laugh.

"Enough of the googly eyes." Christian shook his head. "Kelly, can we talk?"

Alyssa and Sophie immediately started making smooching sounds, and Nick and Brandt hooted. Nothing like being best friends with a pack of bratty school kids.

"You guys are children. Go play with some balloons or something." Kelly giggled. "Let's go talk inside."

"Yeah." Her slender hand gripped his, and they strolled to the meditation room.

Chapter 24

Kelly clung to Christian's hand because her feet were floating three inches off the ground. Never in a million years could she have imagined him shedding his reserve like that. Had he really declared his feelings to the entire crowd? Her skin tingled where their hands were joined, and her heartbeat galloped in her chest.

When they entered the familiar room, Christian released her hand to grab two meditation bolsters. She inhaled an unsteady breath and released it slowly. He tossed them on the floor and captured her hands in his, and together they sat facing each other. The noise from the revelry in the courtyard faded to a soothing silence.

"So." Her throat tightened, and words eluded her.

"So." He drew their joined hands toward him and brushed his firm lips along her knuckles.

She shivered, and goose bumps traveled from her fingertips to the nape of her neck. "Remember the first time we were in this room?" she asked. He'd looked adorably out of place at his inaugural meditation session.

"How could I forget the night you asked me out?" He caressed his thumb along the palm of her hand and flashed his straight white teeth.

"I didn't ask you out. It was more of a friendly visit to go see dogs." She struggled to focus on the words instead of the warmth of his hands. Their physical chemistry wasn't in question, but the alignment of their hearts and minds needed to be defined. Nothing less would do.

He laughed and quirked a brow. "Come on. You're under oath, counselor. Isn't it true that you were so mesmerized with my meditation skills, you had to spend more time with me?"

"Leading the witness." She laughed. "The truth is, Major Wolfe, neither of us was actually meditating that night. I'll admit it."

"I admit it too. All I could focus on was you across the room from me." He hesitated for a moment. "And I also have to confess all I've been thinking about since we've been apart is you."

Her heart contracted in her chest. "Really?"

"Yeah, really. But before I go on, tell me if you want to hear me out. I didn't leave you much choice out there on stage, so I want to make sure you have a choice now. Have you moved on?" He lowered his dark brows, and his smile dimmed.

"Do I look like I've moved on?" This time she kissed *his* knuckles, enjoying the sharp hiss of his breath.

"Are you sure?" Vulnerability shadowed his eyes.

She nodded.

"Okay. I've been working on my crap. I've been seeing this therapist who looks like Angela Lansbury, and she knows how to read me just like a sleuth. We're discussing what happened on my tours in the Middle East, and it's helping me release some of the guilt. Being a soldier will always be a part of me, and I'm a work-in-progress. There's no guarantee I'll be cured, whatever that means. The scars don't just disappear."

He started to pull away from her, but she gripped his fingers in hers and shook her head.

"Christian, believe me, I get it about the scars. Mine run deep and will always be a part of me." Her brother would always live in her heart.

"You're perfect just how you are. Your past simply makes you more beautiful. Don't you know that? It's part of you." His eyes shimmered with a warm golden glow.

"It's the same with you. I heard the most beautiful quote, and it resonated with me so much. Have you heard the one about when Japanese mend broken objects?"

"No."

"It's from an artist named Barbara Bloom. 'When the Japanese mend broken objects, they aggrandize the damage by filling the cracks with gold. They believe that when something's suffered damage and has a history, it becomes more beautiful.'" She beamed at him.

"Babe, that's incredible. You're the most beautiful, vibrant woman I've ever met. But the reason I'm so crazy about you is your inner strength, your honesty, your ability to be true to yourself. You blow me away with that incredible brain of yours and your compassionate heart even with how tough your family life was. I was too stupid to see you were just being kind. I'm sorry for reacting like such a jerk." He squeezed her hands tighter.

"I don't know what to say." A glow spread from her heart, warming her from head to toe, and a wave of calm washed over her.

"Can you forgive me for how I acted?"

"I can forgive you, but can you accept that if I offer help, it's a gesture of caring, and nothing more?" He needed to be able to accept assistance.

"Yeah, that's one thing I'm working on. I can't promise it will be easy for me to be vulnerable, but I want to try." His green-gold gaze remained locked with hers.

"Trying works. So can you accept that the stuff with my brother and my parents may never be totally resolved? I didn't have the chance to tell you, but my dad called me and asked for my help. The Hexaun case blew up and he discovered I'd been right and he apologized." She huffed out a sigh. She still couldn't believe the scene in her father's office.

"Great news. From what you shared about him, it sounds like a big deal."

"Yes. Then he admitted he and my mom hadn't handled my brother's issues well. Things became surreal when he actually told me he was proud of me and he loved me." She shook her head at the memory.

"Have you seen him again?" His voice was gentle.

"No. I don't think we'll all of a sudden become a sitcom family, but we've spoken on the phone a few times. The litigation will take years for the pharmaceutical company, and he's working on removing himself as counsel of record."

"And personally?"

"I just accepted he did the best he could. But I want the opposite. I want a relationship with someone who can admit their feelings, who can be affectionate and warm, and who appreciates me for who I am. I won't settle for less." She bit her lip and looked down at her hands. She would be true to herself.

He pressed her hands again. "Kelly."

She met his gaze and allowed him to tug her closer. His mouth met hers in a soft sweet kiss.

"You deserve the best and should never settle. I can't give you any guarantees. The therapist I'm seeing told me I could move past the anxiety and nightmares, or it might be something I've got to deal with forever. What's different is I've accepted it and know I'll do everything in my power to be the healthiest man I can. So if you are willing to give me another chance, I promise I won't send you away again like I did after the earthquake and after the nightmare. Is that enough for you?"

"Well, it all depends." Her stomach performed a slow flip and roll.

"Depends?" He leaned back and raised his eyebrows.

"It all depends on the feelings between us. You haven't given me the words. What do you want?"

"Kelly, this is new for me. I went to the Middle East when I was twenty-three and haven't been in a long-term relationship. I want to be the man who deserves you." He inhaled sharply. "I am in love with you."

Her belly flip-flopped again. "Christian, I—"

"Wait, let me finish. I love you and I want to commit to you. I want to be exclusive with you, spend as much time with you as you'll let me, show you how much I love you and promise to be the best man I can be. Build a future with you. All of it."

She crossed the short distance onto his bolster, wrapped her arms around his strong neck, and tumbled them both back onto the floor. "Kiss me."

He clasped her head in his hands and drew her down to him. Gently. Tenderly. In between kisses, he asked, "Does that mean you want me too?"

She leaned back and propped her forearms on his chest. "Yes, that's exactly what it means. I love you, Christian Wolfe. Yes, I promise to be true to myself and to you. Together we'll figure it out."

He captured her lips with his and the time for words ended. She wrapped her arms around his strong tanned neck and dove into the passionate kiss with all her love behind it.

A loud knock interrupted them.

"What?" Christian barked.

"Come on, you crazy kids," Sophie called from outside the door, laughter lacing her tone. "The party is still going on, and I think Kelly's boss is looking for her. You might want to, ahem, meditate together later."

Reluctantly, she drew her head back and gazed down at him. "So?"

"Hum." He rolled them over and pulled her to her feet.

"We're always getting interrupted. Maybe we can finish this up later somewhere more private?" She smoothed back her hair and smiled up into his eyes.

"My house is yours. Seven o'clock?" He wrapped one muscular arm around her waist and drew her in close.

"Seven o'clock sharp."

Hand in hand, they returned to the party.

A word about the author...

Claire Marti started writing stories as soon as she was old enough to pick up pencil and paper. After graduating from the University of Virginia with a BA in English Literature, Claire was sidetracked by other careers, including practicing law, selling software for legal publishers, and managing a nonprofit animal rescue for a Hollywood actress.

Finally, Claire followed her heart and now focuses on two of her true passions: writing romance and teaching yoga. She teaches yoga at studios, online for the international website www.yogadownload.com.

Her debut novel, Second Chance in Laguna, won best unpublished contemporary romance in the Molly and third place in the Maggie.

Claire is a member of the Romance Writers of America and the San Diego Romance Writers.

http://www.clairemarti.com

Thank you for purchasing
this publication of The Wild Rose Press, Inc.
For other wonderful stories of romance,
please visit our on-line bookstore at
www.thewildrosepress.com.

For questions or more information
contact us at
info@thewildrosepress.com.

The Wild Rose Press, Inc.
www.thewildrosepress.com

To visit with authors of
The Wild Rose Press, Inc.
join our yahoo loop at
http://groups.yahoo.com/group/thewildrosepress/

CPSIA information can be obtained
at www.ICGtesting.com
Printed in the USA
BVHW041154240121
598599BV00040B/896